THE WINTER

HUSBAND

Lisa Ann Verge

Also by Lisa Ann Verge

King's Girls Series
HEAVEN IN HIS ARMS
THE WINTER HUSBAND

The Celtic Legends Series
TWICE UPON A TIME: Book One
THE FAERY BRIDE: Book Two
WILD HIGHLAND MAGIC: Book Three
THE CELTIC LEGENDS SERIES: BOX SET
THE O'MADDEN: A Novella

Stand Alone Historical Romance
HER PIRATE HEART
SING ME HOME
THE CAPTIVE KNIGHT
ROMANTIC JOURNEYS COLLECTION: BOX SET

Writing as Lisa Verge Higgins

THE PROPER CARE AND MAINTENANCE OF
FRIENDSHIP
ONE GOOD FRIEND DESERVES ANOTHER
FRIENDSHIP MAKES THE HEART GROW
FONDER
RANDOM ACTS OF KINDNESS
SENSELESS ACTS OF BEAUTY

About *The Winter Husband* and the *King's Girls Series*

The stories in the King's Girls Series are inspired by real events. For those interested, here's the history behind the novels.

In 1663, the tiny, just-burgeoning colony of Quebec was dominated by rowdy young men in search of exploration and adventure, much to the chagrin of their French King, who had bigger ambitions.

To settle his far-roaming countrymen, King Louis XIV chose young women from orphanages and the French countryside, girls he honored by calling them his daughters. He gifted them dowries appropriate to frontier life and then shipped them off to present-day Canada to be married.

Eight hundred women sailed to the unbroken wilderness between 1663 and 1673. Known as *Filles du Roi*, they are now the honored maternal ancestors of a large portion of modern-day, French-speaking Quebecois.

Their stories are true—mine are fiction, inspired by their courage, boldness, and spirit.

Publishing History

Print edition published by Bay Street Press
Copyright © 2022 Lisa Ann Verge
Cover design by The Killion Group

CHAPTER ONE

Marie was never going to marry. No matter how many men her jailors threw at her.

"I'm sorry, sir." She dropped her gaze from the bearded young man standing before her. "You honor me with your proposal, but I must decline."

The suitor mumbled a polite word and then shuffled away to the next girl. Marie took a hurried sip from a pewter cup and struggled to gather her wits. If the wine weren't so sharp, her blue brocade dress so itchy, and her ears ringing with voices, she'd think this was a mad, mad dream. The candlelit room swarmed with deerskin-clad men, many with knives shoved beneath their belts. Among them stood a dozen women, scrubbed pink, wearing ribbons in their hair. It felt like a bawdy house, not the home of Quebec's most respected hostess, where unmarried men had been invited to select a bride, fresh off the boat from France.

By all that was holy, how did she ever get to this strange place? She squeezed her eyes shut, wishing herself back in the Paris orphanage where she grew up, sitting in a quiet nook, reading sonnets...until the reek of wig pomade and clearing of a male throat broke the spell.

She braced herself. Two suitors stepped up dressed in coats of velvet and silver braid. The younger one coolly perused the room. The elder fixed an eye on her.

"My dear lady," the elder began, jutting out a foot as he bowed, "dare I ask such a goddess for an introduction?"

"I am honored, sir." After five proposals, she'd written herself a script. "But I beg you to find a kinder welcome among the more worthy women in this room."

"But it is you who intrigues me, *belle petite*." His smile stretched. "I speak with Mademoiselle Marie-Suzanne Duplessis, I presume?"

She dipped a weary nod.

"Excellent, I have found you." He placed a hand on his chest. "I am Hugo Landry, and this is my cousin, Claude Fortin."

The younger man shifted his attention. One eye was milky and blind, the other as sharp as a dagger. She suppressed a flinch. Madame Bourdon had warned her: Everything was wild in this new country, the flowers as well as the men.

"Sirs," she ventured through a tight throat, "I must recommend you to the other ladies, where your honorable attentions will be most welcome—"

"No need to play the coy maiden, my dear." Mr. Landry's lips split to show a blackened canine. "I assure you, we are not triflers, nor settlers in one-room huts like so many of the men in this room. My cousin and I are businessmen here in Quebec, with interests also in Montreal. We soon expect to be granted a large landholding of our own."

"Which makes it all the more urgent that you speak to the others." She might as well have a tag on her wrist, a price written in ink. "And quickly, before they're all spoken for."

"My, my." Landry reared back, pointing one toe to show off his fine leather boots. "Do I look like a farmer with dirt under my fingernails, seeking a common cow to milk?"

To milk?

"In my home," he persisted, "I will need a woman of good blood and fine breeding. From what our dear hostess Madame Bourdon has told me, the only woman in this room who matches that description is you."

"Oh, but you are mistaken." She tightened her grip on the cup. "Quite misinformed."

"Are you not the grand-niece of a baron?"

Ah, Madame Bourdon, you couldn't keep that to yourself?

"I'm a twig far from the root of the tree, sir. I never met the baron." He'd never bothered with her, not even after her father died. "I grew up far from his barony, in a common orphanage."

"Yet the blood runs strong. I see it in the delicacy of your features."

"The delicacy of my features will not bring any wealth to your landholding. For cows...or anything else."

He barked a laugh. "And yet *you* are the only wealth I seek."

"Spoken like a true gentleman." Every word slid slick off his tongue. "Please understand, sir. You look at me and see a King's Daughter. So you assume that I, like every other woman here, has a dowry granted by the king. But the fortune the king gave me is forever lost."

"Mademoiselle, I would take a baron's grand-niece as a wife if you brought nothing more than the clothing on your back." He paused, snickered. "Even better without."

She examined the wine swirling in the bottom in her cup, irritation rising. Most suitors would have sensed her resolve and moved on. This Mr. Landry was leaving her no choice but to speak her shame. "Don't put much faith in my good blood, sir. Surely, you know I spent the last week in a Quebec jail."

"Indeed." His smile went sly. "We have heard much about your troubles with the law."

"Troubles" hardly described her situation. She was no longer wearing iron restraints, but even now, in this lovely, perfume-scented room, she was just as good as shackled.

"In my eyes, lawlessness adds to your appeal. You've become famous in Quebec, did you know? In taverns, many speak your name. They've even given you a nickname."

Her throat tightened. She'd been called many names in the past year. To think, as a child, she used to ride a rope swing behind her father's lovely house without a care in the world. To think she'd once been innocent and happy in a convent orphanage, before all this mortification.

Fortin ignored her silence and persisted. "Usually, these nicknames are spoken in a vulgar local tongue. These settlers live so much among the tribes, my dear, they know their many languages. Would you like to know your nickname?"

No.

"Chepewéssin." The word tripped on his tongue. "It means 'The Northeast Wind.'"

Goodness.

Was that all?

"It's the kind of wind that blows hard in winter, my dear. Because your temperament is so cold."

She made a mask of her face. What kind of man thought malice was a form of wooing?

"Cousin, look at that blush." Landry took a step back, as if she were a painting he'd just nailed to the wall. "Look at the curve of that jaw, that lush black hair. A man could lose his hands in such a mane. Surely there'll be no better choice for my wife. Such studied restraint, such pure blood, and such good breeding—"

"Enough." She set her cup on the table hard enough to make it slosh up against her palm. "Whenever I hear talk of 'good breeding,' I am overwhelmed by the stink of manure."

"Ah." He cocked his head. "The lady has spirit."

"Sirs, I will not marry—"

"Yes, yes, so you say, but the choice is not entirely your own, is it? Your jailers may make that choice for you." Fortin paused as a sudden disturbance in the room drew his attention. "What the devil is going on?"

Murmuring rippled through the crowd as a newcomer stepped up to the parlor doorway, tilting his head under the lintel to enter. Marie glimpsed epaulets, a military sash, and a squared-jawed face of supreme authority. A soldier of some rank, she assumed, from the reaction he'd caused. She was grateful for the interruption, as she was about to cause her own disruption by tossing the dregs of her wine into the face of Mr. Landry. Now, peeling her fingers off the rim of the cup, she watched the newcomer exchange a few words with Madame Bourdon. A lock of sun-streaked hair fell across his forehead as he bent to listen, and then straightened to make a visual sweep of the salon.

His perusal stopped on her.

Startled, she took a step back. The soldier strode through the parted crowd in her direction, only to be stopped by the milky-eyed cousin who bit off a curse as he stepped in front of her.

"You. And you." The soldier's face darkened. "Madame Bourdon should not have let in either of you."

"We're to be landholders." Mr. Landry gestured to her. "And we've already chosen a proper aristocrat for a bride."

"You have no land to offer." The newcomer's deep bass voice shook the timbers. "The government has made a choice. The land you hoped for has been assigned to me."

"Nonsense." Landry drew himself up on his red heels. "I have been told by respectable men on good authority—"

"And I have been told by Jean Talon, the Intendant of New France himself." The giant's nostrils flared. "It is done."

"So you say." Mr. Landry frowned. "I have no knowledge of this."

"Ask him yourself." The soldier leaned forward. "Talon would never grant a landholding to men who, only a year ago, were sitting in a Montreal jail."

Jail?

Between the men, the air sizzled. Marie flattened herself against the wall. Whatever the conflict was among them, she wanted no part of it, especially considering all the knives in the room and the sword at the soldier's side.

If only the floor would open up and swallow her.

Mr. Landry dropped his voice. "This is neither the time nor place for this discussion. Talon will settle the matter." He swiveled toward her. "My intent is clear, is it not, Mademoiselle?"

A nod would send him away, so she offered it. He turned and tugged his cousin toward the door. The newcomer remained, his attention as blinding as a sunbeam.

She dropped her gaze to stare at the third button on his military coat. It seemed the safest option.

"Some advice," he said. "Avoid those men, and their false promises." The giant twisted to watch the men retreat across the room. "I've seen how they treat their Huron wives. They'll make you miserable."

Huron? Wives?

Her wits were in fragments, she couldn't make sense of that.

"I thank you for intervening, sir." She leaned away from the wall, trying to stand steady on her feet. "Were those men really in jail?"

"Less than a year ago, yes."

"I see." *We had much more in common than I realized.* "But they were set free."

"Yes." His voice rumbled with disapproval. "Not by innocence. By bribery. And the help of powerful friends."

By the love of Mary, what kind of world was this? "It's a pity I have no money and only poor friends. I may never be released from my cell."

"So you're the lady prisoner." He swung his hands behind his back. "Chepewéssin."

How quickly vulgar wit travels. "The men of Quebec must spend an inordinate amount of time in taverns."

"Until Madame Bourdon told me your real name, I only knew the other. I'm here to make you an offer."

Dear heavens, another suitor?

"I'm an officer in the Carignan-Salières Regiment. Recently discharged, about to settle land. I could provide the money and influence you need to be released from jail."

"At the price of my eternal devotion, I know." At least this man didn't mince words or spewed false flattery. "I'm afraid you're wasting your time, sir—"

"Captain," he corrected. "Captain Lucas Girard."

She met his powerful gaze. Winter gray, those eyes. Pale light glancing off snow. "I am honored by your attentions, Captain. But I assure you, you'll find a kinder welcome among the other women."

"Will you not hear my offer?"

His softer tone gave her pause. This man had just saved her from worse attentions.

What could she say without being rude? The polite ones were the hardest to refuse, but she was so weary of this farce, tired of the noise of the room, irritated by the burning rawness forming under the sleeve-seam of her new dress. Was there no easier way to be released from jail than to be married?

How had she come to this?

"That landholding," the giant began, "that Fortin and Landry were offering. It's nearly two hundred acres on the south side of the St. Lawrence River."

"Which I am sure any other woman in this room would be happy to be the mistress of."

"It comes with a knighthood. People will call me 'sire.' They'll call you 'lady.'"

She stifled a snort. Even as the granddaughter of a baron's brother, she had the right to call herself a lady. But after all she'd done, she would never be called a lady again.

"I believe you're trying to bribe me, Captain."

His brow rippled.

"I take no offense, sir. It seems to be how this is done." She sighed and dropped all pretense. "Forgive me for being blunt, but telling the truth is the kindest way to dissuade you. Many responsibilities await a wife of New France, yet I can't cook, launder, skin game, pluck fowl, or make candles or soap. I know nothing of gardening or animal husbandry or medicinal plants. I can't do anything more useful than play the pianoforte. Do you have a pianoforte?" She doubted he did. The only one in the whole settlement stood just across the room. "Knowing all this, what use would I be to you as a wife?"

His gaze drifted somewhere above her. He didn't say a word, but she sensed a lot of thinking going on behind his strong features. And what striking, sun-weathered features he had. Smooth of brow, straight of nose. He'd shaved recently, but not with the help of a barber, if the small cut near his Adam's apple was any indication. Perhaps it was a wonder he wasn't bloodied more. He had such an expanse of throat to be shaved, such a strong neck upon those imposing shoulders. Her gaze wandered down his well-tailored uniform jacket, stretched taut against a solid wall of an abdomen. Buffed boots fit his muscular calves. Slightly breathless, she was reminded of the tales of Gargantua the giant and his larger son, Pantagruel, scandalous stories she'd once devoured under the linens with an insatiable and dangerous curiosity.

"It appears," he said, breaking into her thoughts, "that the cousins did not tell you the whole truth."

She blinked. What had they been talking about?

"There's a condition on this land grant." He turned his head as if in search of words, revealing a queue of shoulder-length hair he'd tied back with a strip of leather. "The land cannot be claimed by a bachelor. The new landholder must be married." Massive shoulders moved beneath the epaulets as he spoke. "Talon won't even sign the official papers until after the wedding night."

For a flash of a heated moment, she imagined this muscled man, in all his nakedness, looming above her unclothed body.

She shoved the thought away. "What you've just told me makes it all the more important for you to find another woman. As I've said to all other suitors, I simply will not marry."

"I know. All of Quebec knows. That's why I'm here, talking only to you. I don't want to marry either."

She'd never heard such a lie. The captain had an animal vitality about him. She sensed it, tingling upon her skin. "Captain, I am not so big a fool to believe that."

"I'll explain." He jerked his chin toward the densest part of the crowd. "Do you know that young woman in the corner?"

She didn't have to look to know he spoke of the pretty brunette. "She'd make you a very good wife."

"Three months ago she was married."

"Please don't insult my intelligence, sir." She and the women had spoken before the opening of the salon. Every woman in the room was single. "Madame Bourdon would never allow that."

"I said she *was* married. She is no longer. The wedding happened, there were witnesses. But a week later, the union was annulled."

"I don't believe it." No priest would allow an annulment after the marriage was consummated.

"You haven't been in New France for long, have you?"

"I've been here for weeks." *It feels like forever.*

"Here, old rules don't always apply. Or they're stretched to fit to new situations. That young woman isn't the first King's Daughter to end a marriage. She requested an annulment because her new husband fled into the wilderness only hours after the ink dried on his trading license. He wanted a license, not a wife."

She paused, unnerved. Madame Bourdon had spoken an odd warning before men came pouring through her doors. *Beware the fur traders*, she had said. *Some will stay in the settlements, but others want only the license and will abandon you forever for the wild.*

She murmured, "Why are you telling me this?"

"Because both of us must marry. And yet both of us want to be free."

No truer truth had ever been spoken. She hated the little cell they had put her in, without even a prayer book to occupy her mind. She hated the silence, the idleness, and most of all, the loneliness.

"I'm offering you freedom, and an annulment." He lowered his voice. "But first you must marry me."

CHAPTER TWO

Lucas had expected a different kind of woman.

He'd heard a lot about her in the taverns, where men talked freely when they didn't have a cup to their lips or a whore on their laps. They spoke of the hunt and Mohawk movements and new trails blazed westward, but mostly they speculated about the King's Daughters fresh off the autumn ships, the rosy-cheeked French women who reminded them of their mothers and sweethearts and the world they'd left behind.

They had called this girl a living, breathing icicle. They'd said she was a winter gale that propelled men away as surely as Mishipeshu, the horned creature of Ojibwa legend, who tossed canoes upon the waves of the Great Lake. She rejected every man who begged for her hand in marriage, which made her perfect for his plans.

"You," she said in a rasp of a voice, "are mad."

In more ways than you will ever know.

"Have you come here on a wager?" Her eyes were as dark a blue as a northern twilight. "Has it become a challenge among you tavern-dwellers, to be the man who tries to marry the northeast wind?"

"I don't gamble." A useless pastime, only for men who relied too much on luck.

"So this isn't a gamble, this mockery of a proposal?"

"It's an honest proposal. It serves both our purposes."

"And how is that? A wife is a man's property. Once we make vows, I'm helpless to compel you to do anything, even wipe your boots."

"I'm a man of my word."

"So you'll forfeit your conjugal rights?"

Her frankness hit him between the eyes. It kicked up the kind of thoughts he shouldn't be having.

"If there's a child," she persisted, "there's no annulment. Or didn't you think of that?"

Of course he'd thought of it. He'd spent night after night planning how to avoid the complications that would inevitably arise. Now, since Chepewéssin wasn't the ice-glacier he'd been told to expect, he'd have to toss out all those strategies and think up some new ones. Right now she smelled so good, he had to resist the urge to press his nose into her throat.

"Consider those conjugal rights forfeited." He braced his feet a few inches wider. "And if it eases your mind, know that I'm a man who doesn't take what isn't freely given."

Her laugh rippled with disbelief. "What a paragon you are, Captain. Are we to live apart, then?"

"Living apart isn't possible." He gestured toward the brunette. "Her husband and many other men have been inventive about wriggling out of their obligations over the years, so now Talon knows the tricks. He's tasked with settling this land, like the English have settled theirs, not have our men disappear into the wilderness to hunt furs every winter. If this plan is to work, the marriage needs to look real for a lot more than a few weeks. I have to take a King's Daughter to my cabin."

"To your cabin?" She grasped her chest. "And your bed, I suppose?"

He imagined her curled under the linens, one plump thigh stretched across the furs.

Damn it. "In my cabin, there's a bolt on the inside of the bedroom door."

"No bolt can hold back a man of your size."

He exhaled hard, his ribs tightening. His most rebellious ensign would know better than to test him this way, but this girl was no underling he could command. And she wasn't wrong about the bolt. One good kick, and he could crack open that bedroom door and steal the pleasure he shouldn't be thinking about. He wouldn't do that—but she couldn't know.

He imagined his size wasn't doing him any favors. Nor was the fact that he'd spent too many years in a wilderness fort with fellow soldiers, Huron scouts, and fur traders. Rough company, rough men, rough words.

"I've given you my word." He swung his hands behind him and clasped a wrist tight. "In this country, a man keeps his word, or his word is wind."

She made a strangled sound. "A fine sentiment, sir. But forgive me if I keep my own counsel."

"Then ask me better questions. Like where and how we're going to live."

"Enlighten me, Captain."

"The landholding is miles from here, accessible only by canoe. It's rustic, hardly fitting for a lady. Parts of the forest that surround it are impenetrable. You'll hear wolves howling at night. Moose roam the thickets." This land would never let a man forget how remote he was from the old world. "You'll see no other soul—" *for months* "—except for a passing Abenaki tribe traveling between hunting grounds."

"Is this how you woo a woman?" Her voice had gone reedy. "By telling her tales meant to keep children abed?"

You don't know the worst. "The place is not without its comforts. The cabin is furnished, the fireplace big. There's plenty of game, we won't starve. But a Quebec winter is a fierce thing, and because of that—" he couldn't lie "—we'll be living together until the ice breaks in spring."

She splayed a hand against her throat. "Until *spring?*"

"Yes." It'll be a battle to protect her from a thousand threats of a wilderness winter. But he couldn't fail, he already had too many payments to make in the hereafter. "I'm telling you this because you have a right to know what you'll face."

She rubbed her fingers below her throat, leaving scratches with her nails. It was good that she was scared—she *should* be scared. But he'd put the fear in her, and that made him a monster. Damn Talon for forcing him into this situation.

But Lucas needed the land, and he'd made a plan. "I'm a stranger to you. You'll want assurances that I can be trusted."

"What assurances can you possibly give me? There are only two people on this side of the world whose advice I trust." She winced and pressed a hand against her brow, as if to will away a headache. "Both are King's Daughters who arrived last year from my orphanage. Genny is deep in the wilderness. We'll never find her. As for my friend Cecile..." She sighed. "No one will tell me where she is. All I know is that she's married to a man by the name of Timbre or Tremblay or something similar."

"I know an Eduard Tremblay." Lucas hoped this girl Cecile wasn't married to the dissolute fool, who spent most of his time drinking in Montreal. "He lives in Trois-Rivières."

"Thank you, Captain." She pinched the bridge of her nose. "Now I know where to run, if I ever escape jail."

Was this courage on her part, or just ignorance? "Forget escape. Forget running away. In a week or two, ice will close the river to canoes, and six-foot drifts will make walking impossible."

"Are there no horses in Quebec?"

"Few enough. You're planning on breaking out of your cell *and* stealing a horse?"

"Captain, I'm already an outlaw."

Had it been foolishness like this that had landed her in jail? "And if you found your Cecile, do you intend to spend the winter sleeping in the same room as her and her husband?"

"Of course not. I'll sleep in the loft or the barn—"

"If they have one."

"A shed, then."

"And freeze to death."

"I'll wrap myself in blankets." Her voice hardened, as did those deep-blue eyes. "I'll build fires."

"Will you cut the wood? It takes mountains to keep a room warm during a Quebec winter."

"This is nonsense."

"Finally, you figured that out." An escape into the wild was suicide. She knew nothing of this country. Why couldn't she be plain and biddable? "There are other ways to get assurances that won't leave you dead in a snowdrift. I'll introduce you to a respectable friend who'll attest to my character."

Her eyes narrowed. "Is he a soldier, too?"

Not a great lover of soldiers, then.

He couldn't blame her.

"*She*," he said, "is the wife of an old friend of mine. A King's Daughter, one of the first to come over from the old country."

Wariness rippled across her face.

"They have five children," he persisted, "and Etta is pregnant with a sixth. She knows me as well as anyone in the settlements. She won't hold back a bad opinion, either."

"Why?" She leaned forward, curls swinging. "Why are you making me such a ridiculous offer?"

"I want the land." Talon's offer was too generous to ignore. Being granted a plot in a growing settlement was always a wise investment. But none of those reasons were the real one, which wasn't anyone's concern but his own.

"This isn't about the land." Marie crossed her arms. The act put considerable strain on the edge of her bodice. "Marry any of these women, Captain, and the land is yours. The real question is, why don't you want to be married?"

"I could ask you the same question."

She stilled. The color washed out of her skin. She turned her face away and stared hard at the floor. Damn, he just asked her a simple question. Why did he feel like he'd plunged an arrow into her heart?

What a muddle he was making of this. He let his head fall back so only the oak beams of the ceiling lay within his sight. What the hell was he doing here, in this settlement, in a room that stank of pomade? Why was he being forced into marriage? All he wanted to do was plunge his paddle into the waters of the St. Lawrence River, push off in the canoe, and leave the stink and bustle of Quebec behind. He needed to be surrounded by the wilderness promised to him, several hundred sprawling acres, virgin forest set far from all human contact. Being away from the settled world was best for him and safer for everyone else.

"Soldiers don't live well with others," he confessed, offering more honesty than he'd expected to share. "On this land, I can be left alone."

She tilted her head in his direction, searching his face as if she could burrow through his skin and bone to the man beneath. He couldn't let her see that man. She'd never agree to spend a winter with him.

"Since we're negotiating, Captain...I want something, too."

His pulse leapt. "Speak."

"I want to return to Paris." Her chin quivered. "When this is all done, and your land is secured...I want to go home."

Realization bloomed behind his eyes. *Of course.* Why hadn't he thought of this before? She'd come here against her will, if the tavern rumors were true. The women who settled here, at least those who thrived, arrived already knowing how to manage feral men, hard labor, and ruthless weather. For someone of silky skin and slim collarbone, the settlement of Quebec must seem like the very end of the world, dangerous in ways beyond fathoming.

This woman didn't belong here.

He didn't belong anywhere else.

He spit into the hollow of his palm and held out his hand. "Marry me, Chepewéssin. Come spring, I'll put you on a ship back to France."

CHAPTER THREE

Marie shivered as she walked toward the convent chapel, but not from the lack of a cloak.

"Etta, take me back," Marie blurted to the woman by her side. "I've changed my mind about this marriage. I'll stay in the jail cell. No—I'll take the veil."

Etta, bless her, had the grace not to laugh. Marie had warmed to this former King's Daughter the moment she'd met her, when two city guards had pulled Marie free of her jail cell and escorted her to the door of Etta's upper-town home. Marietta—*please call me Etta*—had swung open the door, welcomed her with a floury kiss on both cheeks, and then lifted a toddler from her hip to deposit the giggling bundle into Marie's arms.

"*Ma petite*, Marie," Etta crooned in her pretty accent. "It's natural for a woman to get dizzy when she's only minutes away from speaking vows."

"This is a terrible mistake."

"How so? You will marry a man who will be one of the largest landowners in all of New France."

"Oh, Etta. I don't care about his land."

"You're getting the land, along with Captain Girard," Etta persisted, "and that's not for nothing."

"Yes, but..." Marie struggled to think up an answer that wasn't a lie. Etta didn't know Lucas had promised to send Marie back to Paris in the spring...or this marriage would be in name only. Lucas had insisted on keeping all the arrangements a secret in order to protect his closest friends from Talon's ire, if their scheme was ever discovered. "I know you've vouched for the captain's character, Etta, but I can't help but wonder. You really only know him as a charming guest in your home—"

"I never called him 'charming.'" Etta pursed her lips. "I called him a very good guest. Because he ate whatever I gave him, made his own bed, tended his own fire, and never tempted Philippe into that shameful tavern in the lower town where a certain kind of woman plies her wares."

"That doesn't mean he didn't go off to that tavern on his own." Marie was sure Etta believed her own words, but men were crafty creatures. "It doesn't mean Lucas didn't gamble, or hasn't cursed and whored and fought and lied—"

"He's an officer, Marie, not a common soldier."

"The only difference between a soldier and an officer is the color of their epaulets."

An inquisitive look sharpened Etta's velvet-black eyes, but Marie turned away from the unspoken question. Etta had already wheedled from her the better part of the sorry tale of her crimes...but there were some details Marie would never confess.

"*Ma petite*, you are mangling your bouquet."

Marie glanced down at her bridal bouquet, an arrangement of maple leaves and loops of colorful ribbons, haphazardly assembled because there weren't any hothouses in the settlement, and no wildflowers blooming in the late-autumn fields. The bouquet, like this impending marriage, bore no resemblance to the real thing.

"In my opinion," Etta said as she tilted her head, "I think something else is making you quiver at the thought of your marriage."

No, no, no. Marie looked away, willing Etta not to probe further, and certainly not about *that*.

"It's natural to be curious." Etta leaned into Marie's side. "What beautiful eyes Lucas has, yes? And shoulders that stretch from east to west. You'll never be cold in bed."

"Marietta, please."

"Am I not speaking truth? Lucas is a rough kind but, I tell you, there's not a man in this country who isn't. Lucas is wise and thoughtful. I'm sure he'll be the same between the linens—"

"Stop."

Etta's laugh rang in the vaulted hall, but the pretty sound only made Marie's spirits shrivel. Etta was a happy wife, a mother of five children, gloriously swollen with a sixth. From what Marie had witnessed, Philippe worshiped her.

"Be easy, my dear girl." Etta squeezed her elbow. "You must keep faith."

"It's not a matter of faith. I'll never fall in love."

Etta gasped and made a swift sign of the cross. "Careful. Say such things and God will put you to the test."

God already had.

Marie knew she would never, ever be as adored as Etta.

Rounding a corner, she glimpsed a cluster of couples gathered at the door of the chapel ahead, including the pretty brunette from Madame Bourdon's salon. Clutching the deerskin sleeve of her fiancé, the young woman gave Marie a nervous smile just as a colossus separated from the crowd.

A twig from her bouquet bit into her palm. He looked even bigger now than when she'd bartered with him, but he wasn't in uniform anymore. Striding toward her in his fine woolens, he could be mistaken for a neighborhood squire, or a country gentleman, someone who might have enjoyed a glass of wine in the parlor with her father, back when she was a motherless child living at home.

Etta greeted Lucas with a nod. "Captain Lucas. I present your bride."

Lucas bowed, murmuring, "Mademoiselle," then straightened up and looked her over with those sharpshooter's eyes. Though she wore the same blue brocade dress she'd worn at Madame Bourdon's—it was the only fine dress she had—Lucas took in the sight of her with an odd intensity. Her knees nearly buckled. Dear Heavens, what had she done, when she'd shook this man's spit-wet hand?

"Is everyone here?" A priest hurried around a corner, cassock flying. "Good, good,

good. The sisters are already pouring brandy in the common room. We could all use a quaff to warm our chill bones, so let's get on with the ceremony."

Lucas held out an elbow. "Second thoughts, Chepewéssin?"

A hundred thousand of them, tumbling all over each other, but what choice did she have now? She slipped her gloved hand over his massive forearm. Five months until spring, Etta had assured her. Five months until Captain Girard, of the arm like oak, would pay for her passage back to Paris, to her old bed in a dormitory of the Salpêtrière orphanage, near the narrow window where she could lose herself in a borrowed book and watch a sliver of life from behind the safety of convent walls. The air would smell of apple blossoms, tinged with a fecund hint of the Seine. Warm summer breezes would make the branches of the plane trees dance, and it would seem as if she'd never married a soldier in an Ursuline chapel in the wild settlement of Quebec. Today's events would be an outrageous story she would whisper in the shared sleeping room with Isabelle and Esme, Noelle and Violetta, and all the other young orphans who'd never been gripped by the disastrous idea of venturing into the world outside the convent.

Lucas led her into the chapel behind the others, and the rite of marriage began. She stumbled over her responses, came in late for the prayers, and hardly heard the priest's Latin. When it was time to face Lucas to make their vows, she fixed her gaze on his milky-white cravat, slightly askew. She mouthed syllables about honor and love and obedience that weighed heavy on her tongue, but couldn't possibly have any real meaning. She said what she must while itching to adjust the knot, as if, by doing so, the entire world would be set aright.

When Lucas took her hand in his, she startled out of her dizzy dislocation. Tugging the fingers of her glove, he peeled the leather away and tucked it between the buttons of his waistcoat. She dared a look above his beardless jaw and found his expression as sober as the priest's. Lucas slipped a ring on her thumb—*in the name of the Father*—and then on her index finger—*in the name of the Son*—and then on her middle finger—*and the Holy Spirit*—only to settle it on her ring finger and leave it there. The pounded silver gleamed, a new and pretty thing too bright for her hand. She closed her fingers into her palm.

Done, except for the kiss.

Around them came nervous laughter, a shuffling of feet, and a rustle of petticoats. She raised her chin, because it was expected she would offer her lips. The scent of wine intensified as he bent toward her. *So he needed fortification, too.* Would his kiss make her toes curl and her whole body tingle and give rise to the kind of anticipation that could numb a woman's mind and make her do reckless things?

His cheek scraped rough, a prickle of stubble, a brief contact that quickly eased. The spot on her cheekbone tingled until a draft cooled the sensation, leaving her standing with her neck arched, swaying from pulled-back expectations. She raised her gaze to find his face guarded, inscrutable.

His steady gray eyes held flecks of gold.

The sudden bustle around them gave her an excuse to tear her attention away. Lucas tucked her bare hand under his elbow, trapping her fingers against the barrel of his ribs. Did he expect her to bolt as he led her out of the chapel? He steered her through the hall to the common room, where Etta awaited, flushed and gushing congratulations. Etta's husband Philippe, his broad smile stretching the scar that furrowed one cheek, came up beside his wife. While teasing the captain for embracing matrimony, Philippe laid one hand on the swell of Etta's belly with guileless affection. Marie caught her breath and turned away, seizing a glass of brandy as the nuns approached with a tray.

Philippe took two glasses, giving one to his wife. "To the newlywed couple," he said, toasting the captain and herself. "May you find happiness in a glorious future."

Etta gave Marie a slow wink above the rim as she sipped. Marie couldn't help herself. She shot the brandy down like a cavalry man.

Philippe made a snorting sound. Etta's eyes danced with mischief. Against the back of her hand, her husband's ribs tightened. She regretted her haste when her head went light just as the priest made a last blessing over the crowd. Their cloaks were presented. Moments later, everyone was ushered out of the convent into the violet light of a falling twilight.

How short a ceremony, she thought, as a cold wind hit her.

And yet how long the commitment.

In the middle of the dirt road, Philippe swiveled on a boot heel and raised a brow at Lucas. "Fancy a pipe and another brandy, old friend?"

"He absolutely would not," Etta scolded, tapping her husband's arm. "It's their wedding night."

"A night I thought I'd never see." Philippe grinned. The scar on his face made him look wicked in the twilight, but Marie had only seen the man's gentle side. "My wife is right, as usual. Talon is probably waiting for you in the lodgings he arranged for this evening, expecting to be personally thanked for the wedding supper as well as the wedding night."

"Philippe." Etta's voice was a warning.

Her husband grinned. "I'll see you at Talon's office tomorrow, Lucas."

"Early." Lucas's voice dropped to a reverberant rumble. "I intend to sign the papers first thing."

Philippe winked. "I won't arrive *too* early."

"That's quite enough." Etta tugged on her husband's arm. "Our children are no doubt clamoring for supper. Goodnight, you two, and congratulations."

Marie willed roots to grow out of her feet and plunge deep into the rutted road, but with one tug, Lucas nudged her alongside him. Marie cast a glance over her shoulder at Etta and didn't look away until Marie and Philippe turned a corner.

Marie struggled to keep up with Lucas's long stride. The gloaming fell over the settlement, washing all color from the world. They soon stopped in front of a house very much like Marietta's, two floors of gray fieldstone with glass in the windows. On the second floor, one window spilled golden light.

Lucas pulled a key out of his pocket. The sound of the tumblers turning kicked up fresh panic. Had there really been no other way out of jail, no other way back to Paris? She cast her gaze about, searching for…what? Nearby, a stranger dragged a wagon full of wood in the direction of the convent. Another man carried a sack of something over his shoulder. A lady with a basket came out of a poulterer's, locking the door behind her.

"Come inside." His voice dipped low, like he was talking to a frightened child. "Nothing will happen tonight."

She shouldn't believe him, no matter how gentle his words. There would be no getting away, if he proved himself a deceiver.

Swallowing hard, she brushed her thigh and felt the lump stowed under her skirts.

She wasn't completely helpless.

Summoning courage, she stepped through the door.

CHAPTER FOUR

His wife was going to be a handful tonight.

Following her into the rented lodgings, Lucas stomped his boots on the fieldstone floor, less to remove clods of frozen mud than expend some frustration. Shrugging off his cloak, he tossed it onto one of the pegs behind the door. When he turned to help Marie with her cloak, he found her staring down the hall, frozen like a doe sensing danger.

A manservant in brown serge approached through the darkness, candle in hand. "Captain Girard, Mrs. Girard." He stopped to bow. "Your room is prepared, and dinner is laid out in the parlor."

Lucas recognized the man as a servant in Talon's employ. "Cedric, is it?"

"Yes, Captain."

"My wife and I can manage from here." Lucas laid his hands on his wife's cloak, her shoulders flinching beneath. "You're free to go."

The man's face sobered. "I've been instructed to wait upon you both."

"And now your task is finished." Lucas set his wife's cloak onto the peg beside his, averting his eyes from her bare shoulders. "Be on your way."

The man had the grace to look shamefaced, but not enough grace to move. "I regret I cannot, Captain."

For one hot moment, Lucas contemplated seizing Cedric by the scruff and hurling him into the street. Wasn't this situation difficult enough? Did Talon have to send a servant to watch their every move?

"I've prepared a light supper." The servant spread his hands in the direction of a room that emanated faint firelight. "There is a bottle of wine already open. A gift from Talon, with his compliments."

Talon had done his work well, damn it. There was no budging or bribing this servant, or his boss would hear about it in the morning. Lucas glanced at Marie and saw, by her wild eyes, that she felt even more trapped than when he'd put a ring on her finger. So he stepped in front of her in the same stoic, unflinching way did when calming a young soldier about to go into battle.

"You must be hungry," he said, spreading his hand toward the dining room. "After you."

He followed in her rosewater-scented wake, bending his head to enter a low-ceilinged room where a linen-covered table, gleaming with pewter and silver candlesticks, had been set before the hearth. His wife slid herself in the seat Cedric pulled out for her. The servant murmured he would return with supper in a moment and then drifted away like smoke.

Lucas yanked his chair back to make room for his greater size, staring at the utensils and plates and feeling like a hungry giant at a child's table.

She said, under her breath, "Talon sent a spy."

"Yes." He reached for the bottle and filled two pewter cups. "He wants to breed us like a pair of horses."

The table rattled. She'd hit it with her knees. *Hell.* Was it only this morning he'd vowed, for one night, not to be a monster? He held out an olive branch in the shape of a cup of wine. She took it without touching his hand. He shot his own cup back, drank half the contents, and welcomed the seep of warmth through his body. She didn't join him, but set the cup down to stare into the hearth flames.

The firelight glazed her face. He wondered what thoughts swirled in that mind. She was such a puzzle, this one. He only half-believed the rumors. A thousand questions ran through his mind, but they had five winter months to fill up with conversation. Right now, he had to figure out what questions he could ask without making her bolt.

He ventured, "What am I to call you?"

She blinked at him, dazed. "Must you call me anything?"

"After a week or two, 'Madame' and 'Sir' will grow thin."

She shrugged. "I'll call you 'Captain.'"

She had a way of speaking his rank that subtly curdled the word. She really didn't like soldiers. "Call me Lucas."

Her bare shoulder rose and fell. "As you wish."

"What of you? Legally, you're Madame Girard—"

"A name I will not earn."

He knew that. He wished she'd stop throwing it in his face. "I'll call you 'Chepewéssin.'"

The skin around her eyes tightened. She hadn't grown any fonder of that nickname, it seemed.

"I'll answer to Marie." She raised the wine. "Will that suffice...Lucas?"

"It'll do."

Cedric arrived to set a bowl before each of them, a thick slice of bread in the bottom. The servant then ladled a soup of peas, leeks, and game, fragrant with sage. Leaving a loaf of bread, yeasty and warm, on the table, the servant slipped out of the room. Lucas glanced at the hearty fare, and then he looked up at the woman in blue sitting across from him, a woman with ribbons braided in her hair and cheeks so flushed they practically glowed.

He stirred up a spoonful of beef and a safe question. "You must be used to finer food."

She put her wine aside. "Have you forgotten that I just spent weeks in jail?"

Patience. "I meant before that."

"Before that, I spent months on a ship eating hardtack and salt pork." She picked up her spoon. "And before *that*, I lived in a Paris orphanage."

"And before that?"

She flashed him a look. He shouldn't be goading her. But he still couldn't square the faint marks of shackles on her wrists with the dainty way she stirred her stew. He'd broached the subject with Philippe, asking him to discover more about her—how long she'd been in the orphanage, who her people were, why she'd done what everyone claimed she'd done—but Philippe had eyed him with a knowing grin, misunderstanding Lucas's interest, so Lucas had dropped the subject flat.

"If you must know," she began, a twinge of wariness in her voice, "I come from Aulnay, north of Paris. You would never have heard of it. No one has ever heard of it. We lived under my great-uncle's generosity in a small manor house surrounded by wild roses. It had a lily pond in the back garden under an oak tree." She paused, spoon halfway to her lips. "Sometimes I wonder if I dreamed that all up."

He could see her, somehow. A little girl sitting on a bench under the shade. A mischief-maker darting away from her governess to scrabble up the branches.

"And you, Lucas?"

He frowned. He'd dug for information, but he hadn't meant to start a conversation. "Until recently, I was a soldier in the Carignan-Salières Regiment."

"So you've already told me. And before that?"

"I was a foot soldier back in the old country. I fought in Flanders in La Tour Company, now disbanded."

"And before that?"

He took a hard look at her. She didn't flinch.

"Before that," he said, drawing out the word just to let her know there were limits to his patience, "I was the third son of a Balleroy family that had pretensions to aristocracy and not an acre of land to prove it. Before I was born, we'd transferred the last of our lands to those to whom we owed many debts."

He waited for more questions, fixing his gaze on the sweep of her lowered lashes.

"So that's why the landholding means so much to you." Shadows deepened in her lovely neck as she drew a deep breath. "That's why you've taken these outrageous steps to secure it for yourself."

No.

But let her believe that.

"It's a reasonable explanation." She raised her brows. "You could have told me that before."

He shrugged. The less said about this subject, the better.

"Tell me more about what it's like," she said, "this land you want so badly that you'll marry a penniless orphan."

"You'll see it soon enough."

Her nostrils flared. She had a temper, this one.

"Captain. I've seen nothing but monstrous forests since I sailed up the Saint Lawrence River on the boat from France, and I've heard nothing but bloody stories of vicious beasts and violence among men—"

An accurate enough description.

"—so it would be a kindness to your new wife to describe where we're going. If only to ease my dread."

He shoved a spoonful of stew in his mouth and took his time chewing. He wanted her to be full of dread. Fear kept a person alert to danger. It might stop her from doing something foolish, like whatever she'd done to merit a cell and shackles, the marks of which still scored her wrists.

"You say there's a cabin," she persisted. "Can I suppose, then, that there are the usual accompaniments of a homestead? Chickens, perhaps? Cattle? Orchards? Wheat?"

By the saints. Soon, she'd be asking about roses and lily ponds. "There is none of that. The land has to be cleared first." *Maybe.* "This year, I'll mark the trees, thin the ones I can before the big snows."

He'd be spending most of the winter hunting, walking the grounds, waiting for trouble. He'd have to find creative reasons to get out of the cabin, if she persisted in wearing dresses cut that low.

"Will there really be no one around?" she ventured. "For the whole winter?"

"No Frenchmen or women." He pulled his mind back to dinner, and abstinence of all kinds. "There are only a few thousand French settlers in the whole colony. There are ten times as many Huron in the region, but their longhouses are farther north and west."

She blinked. "Huron?"

"Our allies. One of many large tribes who live on this land." He hesitated to elaborate. She didn't need to know the Huron thought him unwise to settle on the south bank of the river, a wooded vastness between the Huron settlements to the north and those of their blood-enemies to the south, the Mohawk tribes of the Iroquois Confederacy. "The Huron spend winter in their longhouses, but other tribes allied with the French follow the elk, moose, and deer. The land we'll be living on is a crossroads. There's a chance before the big snows come that a band of Abenaki or Montagnais will pass through on their way to winter hunting grounds."

"I see." She returned her attention to her soup. "Perhaps that's enough detail for now."

Fire flickered on her dark hair. He imagined pulling those ribbons free and watching the curls tumble down. Leaning forward, he hunkered over his bowl and shoveled into his mouth a dinner that tasted of nothing. The silence was a void he wouldn't normally mind, if it didn't keep filling up with thoughts of the bedroom upstairs.

She startled when her spoon scraped the bottom of her bowl. She stared into the emptiness, as if surprised to have eaten it all.

Cedric's steps sounded from the hallway. "Shall I clear the plates?" the servant asked, already reaching for their bowls.

Marie imagined this was how the condemned felt when they climbed the scaffolding to the hangman's noose.

At the top of the stairs, she saw two rooms on the gabled floor, but only one had light seeping from beneath the door. She entered without waiting for him, in some foolish hope she could grab an advantage, somehow dodge a man who towered over her. She stopped short at the sight of an enormous bed with a rough-hewn wooden headboard, the linens folded down like a dare.

Lucas stepped in behind her, floorboards groaning. The tiny hairs on her arm prickled as he brushed by.

"It's late." From the taper in his hand, Lucas lit two candles on either side of a washstand. The light reflected in the mirror and the water in the bowl. "You must be tired."

She wished he wouldn't pitch his voice so low when he spoke to her. It was confusing, to hear a rumble rising out of his broad chest, rough but soft, like brushed wool that still held flecks of hay.

"Marietta had your things sent over." He gestured to a satchel by a folded screen. "You should change into your..." He glanced toward the screen, where a waterfall of lace and cambric frothed over the top.

A muscle tightened in her throat. "And where are you going to sleep, Lucas?"

He gestured to the bed.

"No." She crossed her arms. "Absolutely not."

"Cedric may knock. To check on…us."

"We're not sharing that bed. You're too big for me to fight."

"You're doing a fine job proving that wrong, woman."

She swallowed hard. She knew she shouldn't provoke him. But she'd been in a room like this before. The scent of beeswax candles. The linens turned back. Her pulse fluttered. Her blood ran both cold and disturbingly hot.

"We won't let Cedric inside this bedroom," she insisted. "You can sleep somewhere other than the bed."

"Where?"

There was no chair in the room, not even a hard-backed one. She wondered if Talon had arranged for that, too.

With a grunt, Lucas strode around the bed and then seized a pillow and tossed it toward the hearthstone. He pulled an extra blanket that lay across the end of the bed and balled it up before tossing it in the same direction.

He looked up. "Satisfied?"

It wasn't much of a pallet. She flexed her feet against the pine floorboards. They felt hard, cold, and unforgiving.

She nodded anyway.

"Then let's get this evening over," he said. "We're rising at first light."

Marie sidled by him and stepped behind the flimsy protection of the privacy screen. Lucas rustled about, his tremendous shadow dancing upon the walls and ceiling. She patted her chest, mind spinning. If Lucas spoke true that Cedric might check on them, then she couldn't sleep in her dress. But she absolutely, positively would *not* wear the frothy cambric shift Etta had left for her either. Just thinking of stepping out into Lucas's gaze wearing nothing but this wisp of clothing... To the devil with that temptation. She would undress no further than her corset and linen shift.

Once undressed, she peeked over the top of the privacy screen to see if it was safe to emerge. Lucas stood by the hearth, limned by the firelight. He'd discarded his coat and cravat but kept on his shirt, breeches, and boots. The ties of his shirt dangled free, exposing a hard-planed, V-shaped stretch of a chest that looked carved from gold.

Willing away a rush of warmth, she pressed her forehead against the wood frame of the screen. Her pulse raced. Her own body was betraying her intentions. But she knew better than to let down her guard.

She waited until Lucas bent over to fix his pallet before emerging from behind the screen to dash toward the bed. Climbing onto the edge, she glanced over to find herself caught in the silver net of his gaze. Her heart tripped, beat, and tripped again as he looked her over from tip to tail.

Fumbling with the blankets, she slipped under, the chill of the linens shocking. She drew up her thighs and curled herself into a ball. Peeking over the edge—she had to, didn't she, so she could defend herself, if necessary?—she watched as Lucas lowered himself to a sitting position. He shook back a fall of hair, the firelight playing among the lighter blond strands. The looseness of it made him look younger, less severe, but also more wild in a way she shouldn't be thinking about. He set a pillow beneath his neck before lying back, stretching out the ripples of his abdomen.

The room settled into a silence broken only by the crackle of the fire and faint whistle of wind picking up outside. *Is this it, then?* Would they just sleep until morning? She could feel the pulse of her blood through her entire body, swift with an unholy brew of unease and anticipation. She muffled her breathing and flexed her hands while every pop of the floorboards startled her, every shift of his position pricked her into awareness.

She suspected he wasn't sleeping either. No one could sleep tensed up like that, the muscles in his forearms bulging, his shoulders bunched.

"By the saints, woman." He lifted his head to adjust the pillow. "I can hear your thoughts from here."

"I don't hear you snoring either."

"Close your eyes."

Close her eyes? He *would* want her blind so he could take her by surprise. She turned this way and that. How could he lie there so still, as if the walls didn't crackle with suspense, the very air didn't weigh them down?

She blurted, "You could take your boots off, you know."

"I could."

He made no move to do so.

"It's uncivilized," she said, "to sleep in your boots."

He lifted his head. "Do you really want me in stockinged feet?"

"In case Cedric comes knocking." Her jaw tightened. "Yes."

"But then *you* won't hear me coming."

She caught her breath. Did he really just say that?

"You can't sleep," he rumbled in that unnervingly warm tone, "because you think I'm waiting until you doze off. Then I'll attack."

"I am not." She tugged the blanket higher, though it was clearly worthless as a shield to her thoughts. "You'll get mud on that blanket wearing boots," she retorted. "That's all I was thinking."

"You won't be doing the laundry."

"Somebody will." She thought of her friend Genny, a laundress, who'd come to Quebec willingly and run off into the wild with her husband.

A husband who loved her.

"Take off your boots," she repeated. A dry prickling began behind her eyes.

Lucas sighed. "Marie, you're giving me no choice."

For a big man, Lucas could move fast. He crossed the room in a blink. She scrabbled for the covers, but he grabbed them first and yanked. Cold air swept over her legs, bare below the hem of her shift. By reflex, she slapped her hand against her thigh. His hand followed, as he engulfed her fingers in rough warmth.

He peeled her hand away to examine what she was hiding and then turned his sharp gaze on her.

"A knife, Marie?"

She shook her head, denying what could no longer be hidden.

"You're the great-niece of a baron." He tapped the leather sheath in disbelief. "Armed like a cutpurse."

"I wouldn't have used it. Unless I needed to. You weren't supposed to see it—"

"Your shift rode up when you climbed into bed."

Her pulse leapt. What else had he noticed when she'd shot half-naked across the room?

"Was this your plan?" He leaned in on a cloud of wood smoke and starched linen. "Widowhood would be easier than waiting for an annulment."

"Don't be ridiculous." There was no air between them. "I'm no murderer."

"Good to know."

"I keep it to *defend* myself." There was no evading those sharpshooter eyes. "When I have it…I feel safe."

He jerked away as suddenly as he'd approached. "Pull up those covers."

Her shift had bunched high, leaving her thighs bare to the light. She scrambled for the linens.

"Remember that I let you keep the dagger." He lay back down on the pallet. "But it damn well better stay sheathed."

CHAPTER FIVE

Lucas stood at the foot of the bed, watching his wife sleep. Dark hair cascaded over the pillow. The tip of her nose had gone pink from the morning chill. Her breathing was the only sound in the room, now that the night's fire had settled into coals. He couldn't stop listening to those soft exhalations.

He wasn't sure why.

"Wake up, Marie."

She stirred at his voice, a frown between her brows, but her lashes didn't flutter. He shifted his weight, hesitating when he shouldn't. The canoe was already packed and ready at the riverside outside Philippe's warehouse. If he didn't haul her out of these lodgings soon, they'd never make it to his cabin before sunset. They'd be forced to pitch camp on the banks of the St. Lawrence overnight, sleeping a hell of a lot closer to each other than they had last night. So why was he just standing here, reluctant to rouse this woman who'd kept a knife in her garter on their wedding night?

"Marie." He hooked a thumb in his belt and raised his voice. "Wake up."

Her eyes flew open. She blinked at the rafters, the walls, the blankets at her chin, and then looked over those blankets to where he stood. In the widening of her eyes, he imagined himself reflected, a goliath in buckskin and fringe.

"Don't reach for the dagger." By the saints, a dagger. Strapped to the shapely thigh of a baron's great-niece. "It's dawn. Time to leave."

She glanced toward the window, covered with an oilskin that blocked out most of the light.

"I brought up a tray." He gestured to a jar of milk, a hunk of bread still warm from the oven, and a bowl of gooseberry jam. "Eat well. Once we're in the canoe, we're not stopping to cook a meal."

She sat up and rubbed her eyes. Her hair fell across her shoulders, tousled.

His breechclout tightened. "I'll wait downstairs."

By the time she descended a half hour later, he'd paced a furrow in the hallway. She wore a plain dun-colored dress with several shawls wrapped around her shoulders. Less for warmth, he figured, than armor for her virtue.

"Ready?" he asked.

She nodded and lifted the satchel in her hand. Her jaw was fixed, her face stoic. He hoped her courage lasted.

They left the lodgings and headed toward the lower town. He focused on the sky, on the shadows on the heavy underside of the clouds, and the melt of a light snow on his face. He mentally willed the deep winter to hold up for just a day more. He could paddle his way to the cabin by nightfall, if he put his back into it, even if a heavy snow arrived as early as the afternoon. It was easier to worry about the weather than what the hell he was going to do with Marie once they were snowbound in his cabin together.

As they approached the descent to the lower town, two figures separated from the shadows of a tavern. With a bolt of recognition, Lucas stopped short.

"Captain Girard." Hugo Landry stepped into his path, velvet skirts swinging. "Congratulations are in order, so I see."

Lucas's soldier's sense prickled. The stench of trouble billowed off these cousins, along with the fumes of rum. "Awake so early? Or did you not bother to sleep?"

Landry's gaze slid to Marie. "None of us got much sleep last night."

Lucas mentally cracked his knuckles against Landry's ruddy cheek, but the pressure of Marie's fingers around his elbow gave him pause. How hard would he have to push her out of the way before fists flew?

"I saw you leave your lodgings without your pretty wife quite early this morning." Landry tapped his ivory-topped walking stick against the frozen path. "You headed straight to Talon's office. Am I to assume the papers are signed, then?

So that was what this was about—the land grant. Damn it, Talon never should have gotten these men involved. For all the velvet and spice pomade, Landry was at heart a badger—sneaky, strong, and clever. Fortin, his cousin, was the killer of the two. They wouldn't let the matter go.

He said, "You should have heeded my warnings, Landry."

"I've never been a man to take heed."

"Talon brought you into the deal only to convince me to commit to his terms. It worked. The land is mine."

And the woman.

"I wouldn't be so hasty, Captain. You thought you got the better of me once before, when you marched us to that atrocious Montreal jail." He spread his hands. "And yet here I am, as free as any Frenchman."

Lucas flexed his fingers over the strap of his satchel, ready to drop the burden at Landry's first move.

"Indulge my curiosity, won't you?" Landry's gaze slid to Marie. "Does our lovely Chepewéssin really blow cold?"

A red haze coated Lucas's vision. Landry was baiting him to strike the first blow. His better sense warned him not to attack two ruthless men while a vulnerable woman hung on his arm, while the street was empty, and no witnesses were here to police the fray. Then he remembered the knife in Marie's garter and wondered how well she could use it—

"Lucas! Marie."

Philippe's shout came from behind him. Lucas didn't take his eyes off the men, or the smirks dimming on their faces, even when Philippe raced up to slap a friendly hand on his shoulder.

"I'm glad I caught you before you pushed off. Etta made dinner for your journey." Philippe raised a cloth-wrapped package before shifting his attention to the cousins.

"Good morning to you, gentlemen. Have you come to see the newlyweds off?"

Philippe's free-of-care tone barely concealed a warning. The milky-eyed Fortin must have heard it, or just didn't like the new odds, for he slid his fingers away from whatever weapon he'd been reaching for beneath his coat.

"I see you have powerful friends also, Captain." Landry tilted his head in the barest of nods. "Well played."

"Yes, well, let's delay no more." Philippe patted Lucas's shoulder again. "You've got a long way to paddle. I'm on the way to the lower town. Shall we join our paths?"

Philippe barreled forward. Lucas pressed his elbow to his side to keep Marie safe as they followed.

"In broad daylight," Philippe muttered once Lucas fell into pace beside him. "I didn't think they'd be so bold—or stupid."

Lucas caught Philippe's eye, then tilted his head toward Marie. She had wrapped an ebony-black shawl over her head, which only made stark the deathly white of her face.

"Don't," she said, catching the shared look. "I'm not a child. I saw that one-eyed man grip his knife. We were lucky you arrived, Philippe."

Philippe shrugged. "On the contrary, *they* were lucky. I've seen your husband fight. He'd have gutted them both."

"Philippe."

"The truth is, it wasn't luck, Madame." Philippe raised a brow at him. "Your husband has a history with these men. I have been following them since they first came to Quebec to challenge Lucas's claim. Your husband has had a lot on his mind these past few days, and it's my job to look after his best interests."

Marie's voice thinned. "This sort of thing happens all the time, then?"

"Yes…and no." Philippe offered up the half-smile that had melted so many women's hearts, before Philippe found Marietta and then looked at no other. "You have nothing to worry about, now that you're under Lucas's protection. There are good men and dangerous men everywhere in the world, though I must admit, a half-lawless colony may have a greater portion of the latter."

"I've noticed."

"If I had to guess, the cousins had big plans for that particular landholding." Philippe raised his brows at Lucas. "According to rumors, they've both been spending a lot of time in Albany."

Albany...an English settlement. "Were they selling furs to the English or the Dutch?"

"Illegal either way," Philippe muttered. "Treason, really. If I were to guess, the cousins thought the landholding would be a fortuitous place to set up an illicit-trading station. It's well-positioned at crossroads for both the French and the Huron traders. They could lure fur trappers coming in from the west to sell directly to him, and thus cut off the flow to Quebec."

"Then he'd smuggle the furs inland to Albany," Lucas said, "out of sight of French jurisdiction."

"The English pay well." Philippe tapped the rim of his own feathered hat and winked playfully at Marie. "They do love their beaver hats."

At the bottom of the hill, they approached the silver-gray shore of the Saint Lawrence River. Walking to the laden-and-lashed canoe, Lucas flipped a coin to the Abenaki boy he'd hired to guard it. The boy, one of Philippe's many young, fleet-footed messengers, set off toward Philippe's warehouse for a bowl of sagamité and sleep. Before Lucas could seize Marie and plant her in the prow of the canoe, Philippe laid a hand on his arm.

"A moment, if you please." Philippe made his smile a little brighter. "My dear Marie, if you would excuse us, there's some private business I have to discuss with the captain before he brings you to your new home. I assure you it has nothing to do with drunken rogues starting fights."

She nodded. The tip of her nose had gone pink in the cold. "Send my regards to Etta when you return. Kiss the children for me."

"I will, dear girl."

Lucas frowned at the easy affection between them. Such a charmer, Philippe. He could talk a bear out of its fur and make even the prickliest of women smile.

Philippe strolled a short distance away, indicating Lucas should follow, and then spoke in a low voice. "I took the liberty of adding a few supplies to your stock."

"And on my bill," he grunted, still looking back, noting the line of his wife's jaw in quarter profile.

"Admit it. You haven't the slightest clue what kind of things a young lady might need."

Of course he didn't know what a young lady needed. He couldn't think past the next seven hours of paddling, never mind the next five months he'd spend breathing in little gusts of rosewater scent.

"Etta packed most of it. Needles and fripperies and such." Philippe gazed off in the distance. "Etta also wants me to say a word to you."

"Just one word?"

"You know what I mean. She's perceptive, my Etta, and her advice shouldn't be dismissed. Etta says that you have to understand that Marie is no farm-born country girl."

"I noticed."

Where the hell had she gotten that knife?

"She's been raised gently," Philippe persisted, "and then dragged against her will to a place where neither the men nor the place are gentle."

He flexed his hands. "Get to the point, Philippe."

"Etta suspects that Marie has been…hurt."

The word struck him like the kick of a horse. "What do you mean 'hurt?'"

"I don't know precisely. I'm not sure Etta does either, but she didn't elaborate. All she said was that something happened in Paris, before Marie was shipped here." Philippe tapped the center of his own waistcoat. "She's hurt in the heart."

Lucas frowned. What the hell did that mean, *hurt in the heart?* You had to let someone reach that heart first in order to hurt it. It was hard to imagine such an ungovernable woman would ever offer her heart to any man.

The idea pinched like a belt pulled too tight.

"Also…" Philippe looked at him, with accusation. "I can't imagine how you're going to keep your hands off her through five months of winter."

Lucas tightened his jaw. Why did Philippe assume Lucas was keeping his hands off Marie? Had Marie said something to Etta?

"Lucas, you may be able to fool Talon, but you can't fool me. I know you don't want a wife." He tilted his head toward Marie. "I know she doesn't want a husband, too. You two aren't behaving like you spent the night in sweaty abandon either."

Only in my dreams.

Lucas turned back to his wife, who stood by the riverbank, the wind toying with the folds of her skirts. "Should I bind her to a man she doesn't want, to a world she hates, and a situation she doesn't yet understand?"

"Ah, so it is true." Philippe shook his head. "I admire your sense of honor, Lucas…but Etta will be disappointed."

"She shouldn't be. I'm giving Marie what she wants." No use keeping secrets now. "I made Marie a promise. She gets a berth on a ship back to Paris come spring, and I get land without a wife. We both achieve what we want."

"Good luck keeping that promise, my friend. So," Philippe said, changing the subject. "I suppose you want me to keep an eye on Landry and Fortin in your absence?"

Lucas nodded, not trusting his words.

"There's not much they can do over the winter but scheme," Philippe added, "but I'll keep ears in the taverns, and I'll put extra eyes on them during the spring melt when the river opens up."

Lucas nodded.

"You're a good man, Lucas." Philippe gripped his shoulder. "I know you'll do what's right."

Lucas bumped shoulders with Philippe and gave him a hearty pat on the back before heading toward Marie. The tip of her long braid peeked out from the hem of a shawl.

He came up beside her and saw how she looked askance at the birch-bark canoe.

She said, "It's made of sticks and bark."

"It's watertight. It'll get us where we need to go."

And they needed to go right now.

He gripped her by the waist, ignoring her startled squeal. By the saints, he could just touch his thumbs and fingers as he lifted her straight up from the riverbank. Holding her aloft, he splashed ankle-deep into the water and, with one heave, deposited her in the prow of the canoe. Striding deeper, he climbed over the side, shifting his weight with long practice so as to set himself in the middle and not topple the vessel.

She threw out her arms at the canoe's sudden jerk. "I can't swim!"

"Then stay out of the water." He seized the paddle from where it lay in the belly. "If you fall in, the cold will kill you first, so you'd best sit."

She eased herself down to a crate as he swung the paddle over the edge. He dug it into the river silt, pushing the keel out of the

mud until the twelve-foot vessel wobbled to a
float. As the canoe shot away from the
riverbank, he maneuvered the bow toward the
river. She twisted around, watching the
settlement recede, her breath visible in the
cold.

She's hurt in the heart.

With a grunt, he set his sights on the open
water.

Marie gripped the rim of the tree-bark
canoe as she watched the wilderness sweep
by. Once past the granite promontory of
Quebec, she glimpsed a few rude cabins built
in small clearings, surrounded by stumps. She
saw a field dusted with snow and occasional
plumes of wood smoke rising between trees.
But as they continued up the river, indications
of life became fewer and farther between.
The silence of the place hugged her like the
snow-fog clinging to the tips of the pines.

Her hands began to cramp from gripping
the canoe's edge. She let go to test her
balance. The canoe wobbled with every

wiggle, but not as much as she expected, weighed down as it was by crates and sacks and her giant husband in the middle. She summoned up the courage to twist on the crate upon which she sat, seeking a more comfortable position, as well as a chance to steal a look at the brooding, stone-silent hulk paddling behind her.

The faraway look in his gaze suggested he was mulling over something. She had a suspicion it had to do with the knife strapped to her thigh.

"How far is it to the cabin?" she ventured.

"If the snow holds off, we'll reach it by dark."

His mouth shut as if not another word would ever come out of it. Did he just not want to talk, or was he waiting to see if she would explain herself? He was so fixed on rowing she couldn't read him. The roll of his muscles stretched his deerskin shirt as he worked the oar. The breeze of their wake blew his hair from his suntanned face. Overnight, his strong jaw had darkened with the shadow of a beard, making him look rough and unkempt in a handsome kind of way.

She turned her face from him as warmth crept up her cheeks. It shouldn't matter whether he was handsome or not. What *did* matter was that he was nurturing a bad opinion of her. She didn't think she could stomach that for all the long months they'd be each other's only companion. The worry brought a new tension into the fraught silence between them, broken only by the rhythmic burble of the paddle in the river.

"It belongs to Philippe." She dragged her knees up against her chest. "The knife, I mean."

He scanned the far shore but didn't alter the rhythm or the ferocity of his paddling.

"Philippe has dozens of knives tucked all around the house. I figured he wouldn't miss one. So…I found it in a drawer and kept it."

"You stole it."

She winced. Theft was just another crime to add to an ever-growing list. "I intend to give it back to him."

"It's still theft."

She folded her arms atop her knees. It wasn't as if she enjoyed stealing it. She'd made the choice carefully, out of respect for Etta. By the dust that clung to the sheaf, Marie figured Philippe had forgotten about this particular knife, maybe for years. She'd known, too, Etta would have gifted it to her, had she only asked.

But how could she have asked, without raising so many questions?

"I promise I'll hand it back to Philippe—with apology—when we return in the spring." Over her skirts, she gripped the knife in its sheaf. Just holding it gave her mind ease, but, really, would she ever use it? Could she *intentionally* plunge the blade into human flesh?

"Here." She pulled it from under her garter and, shaking her skirts out of the way, held the sheaved knife toward him. "Take it."

He frowned. "You keep that."

"You don't think I'll murder you in your sleep?"

"You didn't do it last night." Winter-gray eyes skewered her. "I know you're no murderer."

"You can't know that." People could hide the worst of themselves so easily. Even Lucifer was pleasing to the sight, so it was said.

"I'm a soldier." With an efficiency of movement, he swung the oar across his body to paddle on the other side of the canoe. "For years, I guarded a trading post in a lawless wilderness. Before that, I fought in Flanders. I know too many of the murdering kind. You're not one of them."

She couldn't dismiss his soldier's experience…but maybe he couldn't see deep enough inside her. In less than a year, she'd gone from an obedient girl to a liar, a swindler, an accomplice, and now a thief.

She hardly recognized herself.

"My father was a soldier, too." She set the knife down on the crate beside her. "He was a cavalryman in the regiment of La Ferte during the Spanish War."

Lucas's chin dipped, a sign, she supposed, of respect.

"You said you fought in Flanders?" She wrinkled her brow, calculating the years. "Did you fight under the Prince de Condé?"

His rhythm paused. "What do you know of that?"

"Newspapers and journals had a way of slipping into the orphanage." Along with secret notes amid the pages.

"Girls in convents are supposed to be shielded from bloody news."

"They are. But I went looking for it." *And many other things I never should have sought.* "I missed my father and his stories, so I followed the news of the latest wars as a way to remember him." Her heart squeezing, she remembered the smell of her father's uniform, folded and tucked away in a dusty trunk. What, she wondered, ever happened to it? Cut down, she supposed, into make-pretend soldier's uniforms for the baron's youngest heirs.

She shook off the thought. "Why did you leave France to come to a place like this?"

"Like this?"

She jerked her chin toward the unbroken forest of the far shore, and all the terrors it contained. Back in Paris, after she'd been chosen as a King's Daughter, she'd made an effort to find out more about the colony. Stories about enormous beasts, brutal, bone-chilling winters, and especially bloody conflicts between the settlers and first peoples had left her terrified. And yet on the walk down to the waterfront this morning, she'd seen dozens of non-French inhabitants, bartering, smoking long pipes, talking with the settlers, and wearing splendid fur robes. And last night, Lucas had mentioned the local tribes as if he were referring to folks from neighboring provinces, like Bretons or Parisians or Bordelais.

It was all very confusing.

As was Lucas's continued silence.

"Lucas? You didn't answer—"

"Why so many questions?"

She startled at his tone. "It's called conversation."

"Best to keep that to a minimum."

"Why?" What had prompted this defensiveness? Was it simply her curiosity about his military service? "Are we to spend five months talking about food, or contemplating the weather, then?"

"Survival depends upon the weather. Wives and husbands talk about little else."

"Are you so well versed in the habits of married couples?"

He squinted toward the sky. Probably to check the snow clouds, or send a prayer to the heavens, though he didn't strike her as a religious man.

"You want to talk, wife?" He jerked his chin toward the marks on her wrists, exposed below the hem of her gloves. "Tell me what you did to earn a jail cell."

She flinched as if he'd thrown an axe. "I've already done all the talking today."

"Rumors say you set a common criminal free from the public jail."

"She wasn't a criminal." *And there's nothing common about Genny.* Genny was the bravest woman she knew. Her friend Cecile was a close second. All King's Daughters, the three of them. Cecile had accepted her fate. Genny had embraced it with enthusiasm.

Marie had just run away.

But Lucas wasn't done yet. "They say you snuck into the jail, switched places with her, and let the woman escape in your clothes."

"You men of Quebec." The idea of keeping conversation to a minimum suddenly seemed like the wisdom of Solomon. "You're all like hens, gossiping over your knitting."

He persisted. "Are the rumors true?"

"Of course they're true." Of all the sins she'd committed, breaking Genny out of jail was the one she didn't regret. "Genny was my friend. She was put in jail because of my foolishness. To make things right, I set her free."

She squinted as far upriver as she could see. The chill air bit the bottom of her lungs. Knowing Genny was out there somewhere—amid the woods with a husband who adored her—was the only thing that made the shame of breaking the law, and the loss of her own freedom, tolerable. She braced herself for more questions from Lucas as the prow of the canoe sliced through the water. She was of no mind to delve any deeper into details. He wouldn't get another word from her.

Not today, maybe never.

The moments of silence stretched into minutes, and then hours. But for an occasional stop on a riverbank to relieve themselves, and a warning to be careful in the woods, they avoided conversation by mutual, unspoken consent. As the river narrowed, she searched the banks for all those monsters she'd heard so much about. She dozed for a little while, lulled by the gurgle of the water and gentle rock of the vessel. Lucas was tireless in his paddling, stopping only for brief moments to lay the oar across his thighs and take a sip of water from a bladder he kept in the belly of the boat, and urge her to drink from her own. The sky had begun to darken when she finally sensed a slackening of pace. She pulled herself up to a sitting position to find Lucas turning the canoe toward a stretch of cleared land on the southern side of the shore.

The keel soon scraped against the gritty river bottom. Lucas clattered the paddle into the canoe and leapt into the shallows with an agility that startled her. She gripped the gunwales as he yanked the vessel halfway up the riverbank. The last fuzzy tendrils of sleepiness fled as he splashed back into the water, reached over the edge, and seized her by the ribs.

She gasped aloud. She couldn't help herself, though he'd done this several times today. He hauled her up as if she were nothing more than a sack of grain. She flew through the dimness, Lucas's stone-carved, upturned face the pivot of her world, before the soles of her boots hit the frosted ground. She flung out her hands to steady herself, but Lucas had already turned away to heft a crate out of the bow.

Trying to ignore the imprint of his big hands on her ribs, she forced her attention elsewhere. In this case, toward the cabin coming into focus through the trees. It wasn't at all like the little wooden shacks she'd glimpsed just west of Quebec. Stone-built, the house was set back in a small clearing studded with tree stumps. The light of a hearth fire flickered from two small windows.

Fire?

Maybe he'd sent someone ahead?

She turned to ask, but he swept right by her, a crate braced on his shoulder. She hurried to catch up, until a sudden creak of leather hinges and a splash of light across the porch brought her attention to the front door.

A young boy ran out.

Behind him emerged a beautiful young woman.

CHAPTER SIX

Marie stared at the intruder as a thousand thoughts raced through her mind. Was this woman a neighbor? Lucas had said he had no neighbors. A sister? Lucas said they'd be alone. A hired servant, charged with opening up the cabin? Marie swayed on her feet, contemplating any possibility other than the one that popped straight to her mind.

Lucas had a lover.

No. That made no sense. If Lucas had a lover, why would he have bothered to marry her?

With a sudden yelp, the slim figure flew down the porch stairs. That high-pitched sound and the churning petticoats stirred a memory in Marie, a remembrance of an orphans' outing on a summer afternoon, light dappling through the trees of the Tuileries, racing through the paths with—

"Cecile!"

Cecile flung herself into her arms. Her laugh reverberated through Marie's memory. She dug her fingers into her friend's knitted shawl. Was she dreaming? The scent of crushed grass and violets rose from Cecile's hair. Suddenly, Marie was nine years old again, torn from her father's deathbed, bundled away into her great-uncle's carriage, given over to the care of a stranger in an imposing black habit...and shaking with fear until she heard a small voice beckoning. *I'm Cecile.* Fair hair bound in a blue ribbon. *If you want, you can have the bed next to mine.*

Marie struggled out of Cecile's grip. Yes, those were Cecile's deep brown eyes, Cecile's cinnamon freckles, Cecile's laughing mouth.

"It's you," Marie blurted. "It's really you!"

Cecile swiped tears from her cheeks. "I didn't think I'd ever see you again."

"But how can this be?" It made no sense they'd find each other across continents, after so much time. "How did you know I'd be at this cabin, or even in the settlements?"

"Your husband sent a message to me." Cecile planted her hands on Marie's shoulders. "He'd said you'd arrived from Paris and would soon be living upriver from Trois-Rivières. He asked if I could get the cabin in order for you." Cecile glanced at Lucas as he swept by, hauling a burlap sack. "Didn't he tell you all this?"

Marie shook her head, frowning at her husband's retreating back as he headed toward the porch to deposit another burden. An entire day in the canoe, and he'd said nothing? Had he just forgotten to tell her? She watched him descend from the porch and head toward the canoe again, his head bowed, his long legs eating up the distance between the cabin and shore.

He didn't catch her eye.

Confusion made a muddle of her thoughts.

"Perhaps," Cecile ventured, "your husband wasn't sure if his message would reach me in time, or if I would be home, or if I could even come." An eleven or twelve-year-old boy sidled shyly next to Cecile, burrowing under her arm. "Fortunately, Etienne—my stepson—paddled me the whole way here, following the map your husband gave us. Even if there had been ice on the river, I vow I would have walked the distance, Marie. I've been waiting here since yesterday, just dying to see you again."

"This is too good to be true." Marie pressed a hand against her mouth. "So much has happened, Cecile, so much…"

"You're exhausted." Cecile pressed her cheek against Marie's and then reared back. "And so cold! Etienne, help Captain Girard unload, would you?" The boy sped off toward the canoe. "My heart's delight, that boy. I don't know what I'd do without him."

Cecile led her to the cabin, urging her up the three porch stairs and through the door into a room that smelled of wood smoke and pine. They hung their shawls on pegs and headed for a large stone hearth. Marie basked in the warmth as Cecile chattered about how she'd worried that snow would delay Marie's arrival, about how lucky Marie was that the winter had held off for so long. Marie watched her, still stunned, trying to reconcile the demure girl she once knew with this woman in wool wielding iron pokers and shifting swivel-arms about.

"But here I am chattering on and on," Cecile said as she speared a poker into a caddy of other fireplace tools. "I'm so often alone I've forgotten how to be among company. Sit at the table, this is done."

Marie did as she bade, dropping into a chair. "It's so strange to see you cooking."

"Yes…well. It's easy to cook in a hearth like that." Cecile set off across the room toward a hutch full of plates. "I haven't visited much of the settlement outside Quebec and Trois-Rivières, but this is the largest cabin I've seen. That fireplace is a dream, and this cabin is a palace."

Marie's gaze had been locked on her friend as if she was an illusion that would soon disappear, but now Marie took a moment to take in the entirety of the room. The walls were made of raw stone, the pitched ceiling of sawn boards. The dining table and ladder-back chairs were smooth, well-sanded, and serviceable. Two lightly broken-in armchairs stood on either side of the hearth. While in Quebec, she hadn't been able to envision the cabin she and Lucas would live in, but if she could have dreamed it up, it would be just like this: strong and solid but skinned of all flourishes.

She counted two rooms, no more. With a flutter of unease, she looked away from the door on the far side, the one that must lead to the bedroom.

"It's much cleaner now than it was yesterday." Balancing dishes, linens, and cutlery, Cecile returned to the table. "When I arrived, it was such a bachelor's home. Boxes of ammunition all about, twists of tobacco on the table, wood shavings in every corner, dirty boots scattered, and about an inch of mud on the floor by the door. But the furniture is charming, isn't it? And this hearth is big enough to warm the whole room, despite the height of the ceiling."

Marie struggled to see the cabin through Cecile's eyes, not through her own worries.

"I want to hear everything that's happened." Cecile set pewter spoons for two places. "But first: have you any news of Genny?"

"I do." Marie wondered if the rumors so rampant in Quebec had filtered down to Cecile's settlement. "When was the last time you saw her?"

"A year ago, when we both arrived here from Paris." Cecile pushed a spoon and linen napkin across the table to her. "Last I heard, she married a man who abandoned her for the wilderness. Please tell me she's all right."

"Bring the bowls and have a seat. This may take a while."

Marie began the tale, going into the kind of detail she hadn't offered up to Lucas. Cecile didn't even pick up her spoon. Her friend leaned closer, her elbows sliding upon the table, reminding Marie with a pang of how they used to whisper to each other across the space that separated their orphanage beds. Her heart squeezed. How innocent they'd been, not realizing those were the best of days, the happiest of times.

"She's in the wilderness with her husband now, which was what she wanted most," Marie finished, finally answering Cecile's original question. "The authorities will never find her, thank heavens."

"Do you hear yourself?" Cecile shook her head. "You broke the law and put yourself in jail! By my heart, this colony does strange things to people."

Marie wasn't sure she could blame her actions on the colony. The wildness was in her, long before.

"But look." Cecile tapped the edge of Marie's bowl. "You've been so busy talking, you haven't taken a bite."

"It smells wonderful."

"It's sagamité. I didn't know when you two were coming, so this was the easiest thing to make."

"Easy?" Marie tasted a gritty grain flavored with flakes of smoked fish and realized how very hungry she was. "This is delicious. You'll have to teach me how to make it."

"I don't think we'll have time." Cecile dropped her gaze to the bowl she was scraping clean. "I can only stay the night."

Marie's hopes plummeted.

"The winter is coming." Cecile shrugged, and the heavy roll of her hair wobbled at her nape. "Etienne and I can't risk being trapped here by the river ice. An overland journey home in deep snows would be dangerous."

Marie pushed down a wave of despondency. "Your husband is waiting, I suppose."

Cecile's lashes plummeted, and so did the tone of her voice. "He's gone west, into the wild."

Marie's gasped. "Then stay! I'm sure Lucas would welcome the boy's help. I would welcome yours. We can see the winter out together."

Cecile shook her head, her throat tightening. "I have to be in Trois-Rivières in case my husband comes back."

"Cecile—"

"I'm sorry Marie." She put down her spoon. "I just can't."

Cecile's voice sounded odd.

Something was wrong.

"But I won't leave until I hear your story first." Cecile mustered up an enthusiasm that didn't quite reach her eyes. "You have to tell me what happened in Paris. After Genny and I left to come here…and you stayed behind."

Marie's heart stopped.

Don't ask.

Please.

"Oh, no." Cecile's voice softened. "I've been so worried, Marie. Not knowing how everything turned out for you."

Marie ducked her head. It pinched to think if Marie had listened to Cecile's wisdom a year ago and just agreed to be a King's Daughter instead of wriggling out of the honor and going off on her own adventures…then she would have come to Quebec under different circumstances. Maybe still filled with regret, but at least not shackled.

"You were right, Ceci." Marie scraped furrows through the sagamité. "You were right about absolutely everything."

"I wished I'd been wrong, wrong, wrong." Ceci's lip quivered, but she bit it still. "I so wanted you to be happy."

Marie's ribs squeezed. She had to change the subject. "Tell me about this boy Etienne, this stepson who has become your heart's delight. Is he like a son to you?" Marie swallowed the lump in her throat. "Does he take after your husband?"

"No, no." Cecile leaned back in her chair, allowing the change in subject. "Like night and day, those two."

"I wager that boy can't give you half as much trouble as some of the twelve-year-old orphans back in Paris."

"It's not Etienne who's the difficult one." Cecile swept up her bowl and stood up to deposit the dirty dish in a basket by the door. "Fortunately, my husband is away from home often. If I'm lucky, it'll be a long, long time before he comes back."

Marie's heart plummeted. An unhappy marriage, then. What else could be expected from a coupling made in haste? "What a pair we make, you and I."

"Marriage is complicated. Life is complicated." Cecile sighed. "But what choice do we have, but to accept our lot?"

The door swung open so fast both of them startled when it banged against the wall. Lucas stepped through, a sack over his shoulder. The boy slipped in from under his arm. With a shove of his boot, Lucas shut the door behind them, but the latch didn't quite catch. He tried again, to no avail.

"Loose hinges," Cecile explained as Lucas tried again. "When I arrived, the door was swinging in the wind."

Lucas grunted and sank his burden to the floor. "I'll fix it later."

"You both must be hungry." Cecile sprung from her chair and headed to the hearth with an air of brisk efficiency. "There's enough sagamité here for the evening and the morning, too. Come sit."

"Boy," Lucas said to Cecile's stepson, who straightened like a soldier. "Fetch two bowls. We'll be bedding in the barn tonight."

Cecile shot Marie a worried look, but Marie was still shaking from Lucas's sudden appearance. The room that had seemed so comfortably large now didn't seem big enough for all of them.

"That isn't necessary, Captain," Cecile said into the awkward pause. "Etienne and I slept quite comfortably in the barn last night. He's already stoked the fire and set up our pallets—"

"You two have some talking to do." He nodded at her and Marie. "The boy and I will do fine out there."

She went all hot-prickly as he looked at her, past her, away from her. Etienne darted to the hearth, took two bowls from Cecile, and with a curious look at all three adults, he followed Lucas out of the cabin. Lucas banged the door closed once, twice, until the latch finally caught. The porch floorboards creaked as Lucas and the boy made their way to some barn she hadn't noticed when they arrived.

"By the love of Mary." Cecile flattened a hand on the mantelpiece. "He's an enormous man, your husband."

An image of him shot through her mind, looming at the end of her bed when she woke up this morning. She pressed a palm against her chest to hide the leap of her pulse.

"But he showed great kindness by asking me here." Cecile pushed away from the hearth and mustered a tight smile. "That's promising, Marie. I'm sure the Captain will be a very good husband."

CHAPTER SEVEN

The next morning, Lucas slapped another log on the stack of firewood piled against the cabin wall, trying to ignore the scene at the river's edge. Marie and her friend hugged like they would never see each other again. The boy, Etienne, waited patiently in the canoe, paddle in hand. Seizing his ax, Lucas tossed it into the barrow and wheeled it deeper into the woods. He had asked Cecile to come here as a kindness to Marie, but now he wondered if he'd only made things worse. Every damn thing he did or said seemed to make things worse.

He worked off frustration chopping fallen pines. By the steady curl of smoke rising from the chimney, he knew she was keeping the hearth fire going, as he'd tasked her to do. He imagined her sitting with her head in her hands, waiting for him to bust in as he had last night, causing the terror that had made her face blanch. He intended to put off returning to the cabin for as long as possible, but when daylight failed and snow began to fall, he made his way back like he was walking against a gale. On the porch he found a bucket of water, a linen, and a square of lye soap. Taking the hint, he scrubbed the pine sap from his hands until his palms were raw. Then, scowling at the effort, he set the soap aside and pushed open the door.

Marie stood by the fireplace, limned with golden light. The sight of her—a beautiful woman in his house—made him scuff to a stop. The room was too warm, the fire too high, and the woman too damn fetching.

"The stew is ready." Her voice, high and tight.

Flicking the throat-tie of his leather jerkin free, he seized the hem and pulled it over his head, leaving him in a long linen shirt and leather leggings. He sensed her sudden stillness. Not used to seeing a man stripped to his shirt, then? She'd best get used to it. He wasn't going to spend the winter walking around his own cabin dressed for outdoor work and outdoor weather, especially if she kept burning through cords of wood. He hung the jerkin on a peg and stepped toward the table.

"Cecile helped me with this," Marie said, filling a bowl. "She took one of the rabbits hanging in the smokehouse and showed me how to chop the meat."

He pulled out a chair. It screamed under his weight. These chairs were made for pretty girls in petticoats, not soldiers who'd spent more time crouched on sturdy logs sharing peace pipes.

"She told me how much water to put in," Marie continued, setting the bowl on the table before him. "I thought to add a few turnips, but she put some herbs in it instead—"

"It's fine."

"What I'm trying to say," she continued, pulling out the chair across from him, "is that

I've been trying my best since Cecile left not to burn it. I swing the arm in, I swing the arm out. But we're not born with it, you know."

"Born with what?" He shoveled a spoonful of stew in his mouth. It tasted of smoke and ash.

"Knowing how to cook. It isn't something that just comes to a woman. She has to be taught at her mother's knee. I didn't have a mother."

"Everyone has a mother."

"Mine died when I was five."

Damn it. He was an ass. He knew she'd come from an orphanage, like so many of the King's Daughters. He might as well have curled a fist over the haft of an arrow and stabbed her with it.

He offered up, "Mine died when I was twelve."

"Oh." Her voice softened a fraction. "I'm sorry about that. Though she didn't have any trouble feeding you, clearly."

"Our cook is the one who fed me." His size wasn't easy to ignore, but it made his blood surge to think she'd taken note. "Her egg-yolk cake was so thick that an hour after you ate it, it lay like a rock in your stomach."

Why the hell was he telling her that?

"Sounds better than anything I ate at the orphanage." She turned her face toward the fire. "They didn't teach us to cook there either."

"I'm no baron." A fleck of burnt cornmeal stuck between his back teeth. "I don't expect anything fancy."

"Then what do you expect?"

He looked at her straight. Her cheeks were flushed from steam, and one fallen lock clung to her shoulder.

His mind went blank.

"Lucas." She straightened her shoulders. "Cecile couldn't possibly teach me, in one night, everything I need to know about living here. So you need to tell me what my duties will be, other than keeping the fires going."

Duties. Right. "Cooking is the main thing. Cornmeal in the morning. In the afternoon, any kind of stew is fine."

"A stew."

"Meat, cut up. Tossed in a pot. Add turnips, if you want."

"I walked into your smokehouse this morning. I don't know what half those things are, hanging from the rafters."

"Venison, mostly. I bought two hams in Quebec but haven't unwrapped them yet. There's some moose, too."

"What in heaven's name is moose?"

He leaned back a fraction. He'd probably asked the same questions during his first winter here, but he sure as hell didn't remember being so green.

"A moose is like a big deer. They hide in marshes. You don't want to come upon one if you aren't hunting them. They can be mean."

"I'll keep out of marshes. So how does one cook moose?"

"Stew."

She dropped her head into her hand. He wasn't quite sure why. He felt like a juggler missing midair knives. As wind moaned around the cabin, he considered what kind of details about cooking could he give her other than what he'd already said. "Back in the fort, we sometimes dug a hole and kicked the still-glowing coals of a fire inside, then we'd bury a pot with the cut meat. By the end of day, we'd dig it up, and it'd be the best stew you've ever had."

She blinked. "You want me to bury a pot in the ground?"

"No. That's just when camping."

"Are we camping?"

"Forget I mentioned it." He may as well be talking in Mohawk to an Abenaki chief. "There's no need to camp. I've got plenty of meat."

If he did decide to hunt, he would have to take her with him. From the way she'd piled the fire, she'd burn through half the stack of wood in the week he'd be gone, and then he'd return to find her frozen.

"What else am I to do all day, Captain Girard?" She looked ready to launch off her chair. "Other than cooking, that is."

He glanced around the room, broom-swept and free of clutter. "Keep the place clean, I suppose."

"Then leave your muddy boots by the door the next time you come in."

He didn't have to glance over his shoulder to know mud and twigs trailed across the floor from door to chair. "You'll have to wash linens, too, when they need it."

"In a frozen river?"

He jerked his chin toward the hearth. "Melt the water over the fire."

"Oh."

She looked away. By the angle of her neck, he realized she was ashamed of her ignorance. An ignorance that was no fault of hers.

"Well, don't stop now," she prodded. "What other tasks await me?"

Spoon in mid-air, he thought of what the native women did back at the fort at Sault Ste. Marie. When they weren't preserving meat by drying it to make pemmican, or skinning rabbits or deer, or tanning or stretching the skins on frames, or weaving new snowshoes, or dying porcupine quills and sewing them on quivers or moccasins...well, there wasn't much they didn't do. A woman who'd never seen a moose couldn't do any of those things, not without a heap of learning.

"I could mend clothes, if I had a needle and thread." She cast a quick glance at his chest. "You've got a tear in that shirt."

He ran a finger through an old split in the linen. He'd known it was there but didn't care about what no one but himself could see. He hoped Philippe had remembered to pack a needle and thread among the packages still piled up on the porch.

"That's all I can do, Captain Girard." She fluttered a hand. "I'm useless to you otherwise."

He looked past her, beyond the gloss of her dark hair, to focus on a random stone on the far wall. Thinking of what other ways she could be useful opened the floodgates to certain ideas, but it wasn't right for him to imagine her undressed in his bed, a willing participant in mutual pleasure. But she was a woman, and he was a man, and, just like the cabin door, the hinges to those floodgates needed fixing.

He turned his empty spoon over and over in his hand, forcing his thoughts straight. Marie could have been a very different kind of woman. After all that had happened to her—all that he *knew* had happened, at least, because this woman hid a world of secrets—he supposed she would have been justified to scream, weep, and complain about her fate. Right now she was contrary and tense, but controlled. She didn't want to be here, but she was trying to figure out the rules. She acted like the kind of greenhorn soldier he would seek out for promotion, someone who could guard their own impulses, use fear as a whetting stone. The fact that she *wanted* to be of some use was promising. If they both stayed busy—if they kept out of each other's way—then they might be able to live together without being together.

Then, as he'd hoped, an idea shot across his mind.

He asked, "Can you read?"

"Of course I can read."

Spoken in a voice as tart as bearberries. She didn't know being literate was a gift. Few of the hardy settlers in this colony could tell one letter from the next, even some of the well-born.

He, himself, had spent his whole childhood struggling. "A man who works all day outside is too tired to squint at letters. You can read to me at night."

She glanced around the room. "Read what?"

"Books."

She spread her empty hands, waiting for an explanation. Didn't she know? He took note of a pile of pillows and folded blankets by the hearth as realization dawned. She and Cecile had slept in this room last night, ignoring the bedroom with its own fireplace behind the closed door. *Hell.* His wife couldn't bear to sleep in his bed, even when he wasn't in it.

It was going to take a lot more than one kindness to make this woman stop thinking he was a monster.

"There's something you need to see." He shoved his chair back. "Come with me."

CHAPTER EIGHT

Marie felt like she'd swallowed a hive of bees as her husband strode across the room toward the bedroom she'd avoided. His sun-streaked queue and its rawhide tails slid against his back as he glanced over his shoulder.

Beneath the table, she fussed with her trembling hands, trying to calm the upheaval both inside and out. Little sparks danced across her skin as she imagined him heaving her up in those tremendous arms, throwing her on his bed and...*stop.* By the saints, her sinful self was betraying her. Lucas's rough good looks, along with her endless, wayward thoughts, had roused an uncomfortable awareness of his muscular beauty. To complicate matters, Lucas's kindness at sending for Cecile had stirred up a whole lot of other feelings. Clearly, he wanted her to trust him. But there was nothing more dangerous than an unexpected kindness from a man.

She stood up on wobbly legs. Her body flushed prickly and cold as she headed across the room. Swallowing a lump the size of a plum, she passed by Lucas and his aura of cinnamon-scent. She entered his bedroom and put space between him and the heady incense.

Her steps faltered. The bed was piled high with more furs than she'd ever seen. She didn't know the names of the creatures that bore such thick, lush pelts. But it wasn't the extravagance of furs that made her pulse flutter. It was the great, wide, sweeping size of it. High like a king's, set upon a platform. Big enough for a man like Lucas. Big enough for a bedmate.

"Marie."

She startled and fixed her attention on the plaited rug under her feet.

"Look up," he commanded.

She hazarded a glance at a cabinet fronted with leaded-glass doors, the kind of furniture that might have been plucked from the wax and leather-scented study of her old home. It struck her as oddly out-of-place. She couldn't imagine why someone would pack up this delicate piece of furniture and transport it all the way into the wilderness. What a miracle the glass had survived the roll of the ocean, the bump of a cart over pitted tracks, and, no doubt, a ride in a canoe.

She peered at the contents inside, and her heart rose to her throat. "Are those..."

"Books," he said. "Yes."

She blinked a few times just to make sure she wasn't imagining. Behind the glass doors, there weren't just one or two tomes...there were dozens. In an instant, she was pulled back to a day when she and the other high-born girls of the orphanage toured the Louvre while the king was off in Versailles building his new palace. She'd stepped into a room so full of bookshelves, she'd died a little, overcome with the craving to touch them, open them, and run her fingers down the spines.

Her hand was suspended before her, the key in the lock within reach. If she tried to touch it, would it all disappear?

She whispered, "May I...?"

At his nod, she stepped closer and twisted the iron key. The glass door swung open to the scent of old leather and paper. Some of the books were shiny, as if the bindings had been oiled. Others were worn and frayed at the tops and bottoms. Her father had owned fourteen books. She had read them to him during the evenings as he'd slumped in a chair, hollow-eyed and sleepless during those last few years, pulling on the lip of his pipe. But this case held so many more, the spines embossed in gold.

She whispered, "Are all these yours?"

"They came with the cabin." His voice rumbled in the room. "The previous owner found out it would cost a fortune to crate them and ship them back to France."

"Why didn't he sell them here in the settlements?"

"The Jesuits didn't want them. Fur trappers wouldn't buy them either. They travel by canoe, and books are ruined in water. As for the settlers...many can't read."

As wind whistled around the cabin, she trailed fingertips along the spines. Molière, Rabelais, Racine, Perrault. As she crouched to read the titles on a lower shelf, Lucas stepped away to peek behind the oilcloth covering the window.

"That's a wolf-wind," he said. "It means a storm is coming. I have to pull the canoe into the barn for safety and stow those packages on the porch."

She couldn't meet his eye. She didn't want him to know how he'd gutted her with this new generosity. "I'll...I'll read to you later. When you come back from—"

"Another night," he interrupted. "Tonight, I sleep in the barn."

Her heart beat out the passing of the seconds. Why would he offer to sleep in the barn when he had this huge, comfortable bed?

Was he testing her? She knew it would be kinder for her to insist he sleep here. She could always sleep on a pallet by the parlor fire in the other room. It would be petty to deny a man who'd shown her such consideration the comfort of his own home.

But the words...wouldn't come.

Boards creaked under Lucas's retreat. She tracked the progress of his heavy step into the parlor as he wrestled into his jerkin and swept the fur coat over all. The front door squealed open on the loose hinges and then bounced shut behind him, once, twice, until the latch finally stuck.

CHAPTER NINE

Marie jerked out of sleep to the feel of a book sliding off her lap. Startled, it took her a moment to remember where she was. After Lucas had left for the barn, she'd brought a book into the main room, intending to read by this hearth and deny herself, as she'd denied Lucas, the comfort of that bed. How long had she been dozing? She shivered as a biting wind sifted through the fibers of her shawl, a wind flooding in through the swinging front door.

Holy Mary! She bolted upright and uncurled her aching legs from the awkward position in which she'd slept. Skating across the room in stocking feet, she winced at the icy floor. Snow billowed through the open door. Fighting the suck of the wind for control, she pressed the door shut until the latch caught.

Inside, the fire dimmed, now bereft of the wind that had blown it into a roar. Outside, the storm howled. The rafters creaked, the stones moaned. Plunged into semi-darkness, she suddenly regretted reading ghost stories to the other girls in the gloom of their orphanage dormitory. Every flickering shadow in this rustic cabin took the shape of a goblin, a demon, a monster skulking.

She shook herself. She wasn't a child anymore. She pushed away the imaginings and focused on how to keep the storm from shoving its way in again. She could brace a chair against the door...maybe it would be heavy enough. She took a single step toward that intention just as she heard the click of claws.

Her muscles seized. Backing up, she strained her ears. Snow fell muffled upon the roof. A board popped beneath her weight. Had she imagined that horrid series of boneclacks upon wood? A pulse pounded in her ears, but not so loud that she didn't hear the second jittery movement of clawed feet.

Clickety-click-click.

Fragments of stories ripped through her mind. Settlers eaten by bears. Fur trappers stalked by mountain lions. Farmers found trampled in the fields. The backs of her knees gave, but she locked them tight. She couldn't lose consciousness, not now. That would make her defenseless. She breathed in. Breathed out. Breathed in again. With the storm rattling the door at her back, she mentally cast about for something she could use as a shield, or as a weapon, and then remembered where Lucas had last leaned his long gun, only a few steps to her left.

She heard the sound again.

Clickety-click-click.

Choking down the horror, she slid sideways, her hair tangling in the hinges until she finally cleared the rattling door. She walked her hand farther along the wall until her palm hit a bore of cold metal. She gripped it, lifted it, and fumbled with the weight. How big was the creature? Could she stun it by hitting it with the wide end of the weapon? Her mind stumbled through ever more terrifying options as the storm blew hard enough to jolt the latch. The door flew open again.

She lunged away before it slammed against her. Embers in the hearth blazed. The edge of the linen tablecloth floated aloft, revealing a ghostly white face beneath. A high, arched back.

Hollow, demonic black eyes.

A scream ripped from her throat. The creature darted out. She lunged toward it and swung the gun blindly. She swung and swung and felt the jolt up her arms upon contact with *something*. She kept pushing, sweeping the unholy thing with maw and claws toward the gaping door, dragging a trail through the drifting snow. She flailed and tossed up snow until she struck something immovable.

A vast shape loomed in the darkness. The world dissolved into terror.

Bear?

Moose?

Lion?

"Marie, stop screaming."

A voice...a voice. Her teeth clanked as she shut her mouth. The gun was ripped out of her grasp. An immense hand gripped her shoulder and pushed her back into the room. The light of the fire revealed a deerskin-clad Lucas, his frown fierce, his grey eyes glittering. Her blood raced like it had only once before, back in Paris, when she had torn through the dirty streets with danger biting at her heels.

Lucas. A choking pressure rose up in her. She couldn't help herself. She threw herself against him, gripped handfuls of fringe, and held fast. His heart beat hard against her ear, sounding like, *safe, safe, safe.* She shook the fringe with her fists as if rattling iron bars.

A warm hand settled in the hollow of her back. His chest rumbled as he spoke.

"What happened?"

"I saw"—she couldn't catch her breath— "a *creature.*"

"Where?"

"Inside...inside the cabin."

Beneath his deerskin shirt, a wall of muscle danced. She sensed him turning his head this way and that, looking around...searching for something.

A fresh wave of panic weakened her. Had the creature she hit been the only one? "I pushed it onto the porch...I think."

His hand abandoned her back. "Go stand by the hearth."

Don't make me leave. He waited tense against her, but she didn't dare move.

"You'll be safe by the hearth." He shifted his grip on the gun. "Night creatures don't like the light."

Night creatures.

Inside.

She loosened her grip on the fringe. The doeskin of his shirt clung to her cheek as she separated from his body. She backed up into the light, hardly breathing. Once bathed in the heat of the embers, she added a log to stoke the flames, willing her stomach to stop twisting, her mind spinning.

Lucas made his way across the murky room. As the flames leapt to devour the new log, she saw him, a mountain of a man gripping a rifle, poking things here and there. Moments later, he strode toward her, the rifle pointed down and away. His gray gaze took in her disheveled hair, her stockinged feet, and then passed quickly over the rest of her. Only then did she realize she was standing before him in a thin shift, with the firelight bright behind her.

He asked, "Are you hurt?"

"No." She clutched her own shoulders. "I got to the...thing, whatever it was, before it got to me."

"You were screaming."

She vaguely remembered that. The rawness in her throat attested to the same. She must have been screaming at the top of her lungs if he'd heard her from another building, and over the wind.

"It had teeth," she said, defenses rising. "I heard its claws clicking on the floor. It was white or light gray."

"As big as a farm cat?"

She shook her head, remembering teeth and glistening maw, but then paused. In her mind, it had already swelled to the size of an African lion she'd seen once, the day the king had opened his new menagerie outside of Paris. But the creature in this cabin had been small enough to fit under a table.

"Maybe," she conceded, rubbing one cold toe over another. "Maybe it wasn't so big."

He grunted. "Sounds like an opossum."

"O-possum?"

"A white forest rat, bit of a scavenger."

"Rats don't grow that big." So maybe she'd been foolish. He didn't have to rub it in. "Even in Paris."

He lifted the gun into the light. "You had this in your hands. Why didn't you shoot it?"

She blinked at him, not understanding. He couldn't be serious, asking that question. She started to explain but stopped. To tell him the truth would be to admit how useless she was. The thought brought a flush of both anger and shame.

"By the saints," he barked. "You don't know how to shoot a flintlock."

She tilted her chin. "I must have missed that lesson in the orphanage."

Lucas mumbled a string of words in an odd, guttural language, but there was no denying the tone.

Was there a limit to the contempt he could hold her in…or she for herself?

"Brace both chairs against the door after I leave." Lucas turned away, his voice gruff. "I'll fix the hinges and the latch tomorrow. For now, get some sleep."

As if she'd ever close her eyes again.

"First thing in the morning," he barked, pausing at the threshold, "I'm teaching you how to shoot."

CHAPTER TEN

The next morning, twenty paces behind the cabin, Lucas swiped the top of a tree stump, sending powder tumbling into the drifts. Yanking a block of firewood out of his satchel, he set it on end and then waded through the snow to the next stump. He hazarded a glance toward the back of the cabin, where Marie stood in her hampering long skirts, her chin tilted at a defiant angle he recognized all too well.

Damn Talon. Damn him, and the nuns of the orphanage, and the administrators in Paris, and even King Louis XIV, for sending innocents to Quebec. She couldn't cook. She couldn't hunt. She couldn't shoot. Talon might as well have fed her to the bears.

And now everything inside him screamed.

Protect her.

He finished setting up the targets and trudged in her direction. She didn't say a word, but her stance shouted, *Don't break my pride.* At least she wasn't making the inhuman screeching noise he'd heard last night, more unnerving than the death cries of fighting raccoons. He'd been outside the barn, roused from a restless sleep to relieve himself, when the shrieking began. He'd raced to the cabin, where she'd thrown herself against him like a frightened kitten.

Small. Trembling. Soft.

"Take off your gloves." He seized the flintlock leaning against the cabin. "To shoot a gun, you have to feel it."

He planted the butt of the weapon on his boot to start the loading process. He did it quickly—she'd have plenty of opportunity later to learn how to load it herself. For now, he just had to get her shooting. Seizing the powder horn hung across his chest, he pulled off the cork, tapped some black powder into the bore, and then replaced the cork before letting the horn fall to his side. Flipping up the flap of his pouch, he grabbed a ball and dropped it into the bore, then used the ramrod to shove the ball deeper. Swinging the flintlock up, he checked the pan to make sure it was dry and then added more powder.

When he finished, she was still pinching off, finger by finger, a pair of gloves better suited for picking up porcelain cups.

"Face the targets," he said.

Her midnight-blue eyes flashed, but she did as she was told, turning to give him a view of slim back. He came up right behind her, leaning to one side to present the gun so she could grip it in the proper position. She put her left hand around the bore and her right hand on the stock in search of a good grip.

He said, "Put the butt in the hollow of your shoulder."

She fumbled with positioning the weapon until he had no choice but to reach around her.

"Right here." He tapped his bare fingers against her shawl and then guided the wide end into place. Her mantle was meant for Paris winters, so he'd made her leave it behind in the cabin in favor of multiple layers of clothing. Now she was swathed in woolen shawls, one wrapped over her hair. It was impossible to keep his body from touching hers and still position her hands correctly. Her head was tucked under his chin. Soft fibers feathered against his throat. As he stepped back and withdrew his hand from where he'd adjusted her grip, he brushed a curve that could only be the side of her breast.

"Cradle the barrel." He spoke sharply, as if the fullness of that firm curve wasn't imprinted on his skin. "Don't hold it in your fist like that. Let the barrel lie in the cup of your left hand."

Such a small hand, cold and pink.

With a grunt, he leaned in to lay his fingers over hers. They felt like icicles. He swallowed her hand in the warmth of his palm, using the excuse of nudging her grip into a better position. By the saints, it wasn't even deep winter, and she could barely suffer this tender cold. If his treacherous eyes hadn't deceived him, there wasn't a lot of extra padding on her bones, except in one place, the swell of which, plumped up by petticoats and all the other nonsense Frenchwomen wore beneath their dresses, now pressed against him in a way that made sweat rise on his brow, despite the chill.

"That's it." He released her hand and stepped away from what he shouldn't be imagining. "Now cock it."

"Excuse me?"

"Cock it." Nervous as a doe during the hunt, she was. "Put your thumb here." He took the icicle that was her thumb and set it on the hammer. "Pull that back until you hear a click."

She tried. Her thumb slid over the top of the hammer. When she made it jump, he slammed his hand over hers, which made *her* jump. By the saints, he was always scaring the wits out of this woman.

"When the hammer hits the frizzen," he explained, "sparks will fly."

"S-s-sparks?"

"That'll light the powder in the pan, which will set off the charge inside. The ball will go wherever the bore is aimed, so make sure you cock that hammer all the way back until it clicks, while keeping the gun aimed exactly where you want to shoot, just in case the hammer flies unintentionally."

He was close enough to hear her swallow.

"I'll cock it for now." He nudged her thumb off the hammer and used his own to pull the lever back. "Did you hear that click?"

Her head nodded in the nook of his jaw and throat.

"Now put your finger on the trigger and squeeze it to fire—"

"The workings are apparent to me now, Captain Girard."

Her voice, as cool as her fingers.

Good. The grit was back.

"Whenever you're ready." He stepped away to give her the freedom to move. "Aim for one of those logs, then squeeze. I should warn you—"

POW.

The recoil jerked her against his chest. He seized her to keep her upright.

She gasped and dropped the weapon. "What did I do wrong?"

"Nothing. That's the recoil." Warmth rose from a gap in her shawl, smelling of woman and roses. "You're bundled for more reasons than the cold. Those shawls work as padding to cushion the hit."

She shook out of his grip. "Why didn't you warn me?"

"You'd have tightened up and made the impact worse."

"Or I could have braced myself."

"You're not my first recruit, Marie—"

"Nor am I a soldier."

"Soldier or not, in this wilderness you have to shoot without fear. You can't hesitate when what needs killing is coming at you fast."

She glared at him. "Just tell me what I need to know before I need to know it."

"Here's something you should know," he said tightly. "This flintlock is a lot like you. It doesn't take much to set it off."

Shouldn't have said that. Shouldn't be goading her. But last night, in the dark of the storm, for one brief moment, she had clung to him. Since then, he hadn't had a moment free of that memory. She'd thrown up walls between them ever since their first meeting. Now he knew how easily those walls could tumble down.

She turned her face away, so he saw nothing but the stiffness of her shoulders and rigid carriage of her head. He couldn't eat the words, so he walked a wide circle around her to pick up the weapon from where it had fallen. The pan was full of wet snow. He focused on swiping out the flakes and drying it. Better to fix his attention on the weapon and not the woman wreaking havoc on his fragile peace of mind.

Finally, she said, "I didn't knock over a single target."

Oh yes, you did.

"There's not even a log wiggling."

"You shot wide." How much drier could the pan get? "You'll do better with practice."

"I will." The tone of her voice shifted. "Show me how to reload."

He paused cleaning to see her squinting toward the targets, one hand outstretched in his direction. Blindly, she waited for him to put the flintlock in her grip.

He should stop underestimating her.

He handed her the weapon, explaining again how to load it, offering the ball and horn. A soldier wouldn't live long unless he could shoot and reload at least three times a minute. It must have taken her ten minutes, fumbling as she did with those pink-tinged, half-frozen hands, to get the weapon loaded and the butt set against her shoulder. She cocked it carefully this time, pulling back until it clicked, and then aimed down the barrel before squeezing the trigger.

She didn't fly off her feet as the shot echoed through the woods. She lowered the bore and peered through the dissipating smoke. "Everything's still standing."

"You waited too long to pull the trigger."

"I was *aiming*."

"The barrel sagged."

Her chin tightened. She turned the gun upside down, yanked out the ramrod, and held out her free hand. "Powder and shot, please."

He suspected she wasn't going to give up practicing anytime soon, so he settled himself against the fencepost of the yard that would someday hold pigs and watched.

Good thing he'd stocked up on ammunition and saltpeter for the winter. She made three shots wide, canting east, and then followed that up with two more shots wide, this time canting west. He suggested she raise the bore higher to compensate for the weight of the rifle and strength of her grip. She hit a knot in a white pine twenty feet off the ground and swore in her lady's voice in a way that made him bite the inside of his cheek. Dinner was going to be late today, he figured, as the next shot kicked up snow about a dozen yards beyond the targets.

She kept reloading. More quickly each time. Now she was doing one reload in less than two minutes, though her aim wasn't getting much better.

As she pulled the ramrod from the bore once again, he said, "You're thinking too much."

Her head jerked up, smacking him with a frustrated look.

He said, "Try staring at the target as you raise the rifle and then pull the trigger right away."

"Don't aim, you mean?" She seized the horn from his grip and tapped powder into the pan, thrusting the horn back at him when done. "How's that going to work?"

"Better than what you're doing now, I suspect."

Blue flames, those eyes, they could light a bonfire. Blasted with that heat, he felt his cock remind him it had been months since he'd enjoyed the warmth of a woman.

Down, boy.

"You're a terrible teacher." She swiveled toward the target and raised the rifle just as she pulled back the hammer.

POW.

Crack!

She peered through the billow of black smoke, then dropped the weapon and took a few running steps forward. The shawl slipped off her head as she stopped. All that remained of one of the targets was splinters scattered around the stump.

"I'd call that a direct hit," he said, hooking the much-lighter powder horn back onto his belt. "What were you saying about me being a terrible teacher?"

He expected another one of those blood-warming glares. But Marie swirled in the snow, her skirts twisting. She looked at him with her hands pressed against her cheeks, her black hair tumbling, and made a triumphant little sound. The smile on her face was like the break of clear white sunlight through a sky full of clouds.

His heart stopped.

The whole world froze in crystalline clarity, dark pines stark against the sky, light glittering off beds of powdery snow, Marie's lips gleaming as laughter fell from them.

The truth hit him like a falling tree.

He would never last the winter without kissing her.

CHAPTER ELEVEN

Lucas spent the rest of the day in a daze. He went through the motions of work, fixing the latch on the door, eating the midday meal, plunging into the woods with a hatchet to clear branches from a felled pine. No amount of crisp air could flush the scent of roses from his head. Returning to the cabin in the twilight, he braced himself for the sight of her. Inside, she strode about the place like nothing happened, chattering nonsense about the stew she'd made, like she hadn't overturned his world with a smile. He kept his head ducked and answered her questions with none of his own. Yes, he was hungry. No, it hadn't started snowing again. Yes, they had enough wood. He wolfed down the stew to have an excuse for not conversing. He had to get out of this house, away from temptation.

When she sat down across from him with all the grace of a dove alighting, he took a last spoonful of dinner and then bolted up from the table.

"Lucas, stop."

He already had one hand on his deerskin coat.

"Yesterday, you asked me to read to you." Marie gestured to a book lying on the hearth chair. "I've picked out a story for tonight."

Her gaze was soft, uncertain. He avoided it by focusing on her long, lovely throat, wondering what that soft skin would feel like under the pressure of his mouth.

No, absolutely not, I can't stay.

That's what he meant to say. But the words that came out of his mouth were, "All right."

A spark lit her eyes. Hope? Delight? The look was a hunter's arrow, a kill shot.

"Sit, then," she said, her voice rising in pitch. "I'll join you in a moment."

He shuffled to the hearth like a damn schoolboy under a pretty teacher's spell. The pull he felt toward her made it hard to breathe. Dropping into the padded chair, he let his legs sprawl toward the fire. He would listen for a while, he told himself, and then use the excuse of exhaustion to leave.

Her skirts rustled as she moved about the room, clearing his bowl and spoon before slipping into the seat at the other side of the hearth. He fixed his attention on the shifting color of the flames and tried not to think about the smile that had unhinged him as surely as a winter squall had yanked the latch off the front door. Pages rustled as she opened the book. She started to read, her speech strained, the cadence awkward, but after the turning of a page or two, her voice relaxed. The tale of the giant Gargantua unfurled.

She sounded rapt, absorbed in the story, so he turned his head slightly to observe her unawares. He'd seen Marie dressed in ribbons at Madame Bourdon's salon. He'd seen her in a linen shift with a knife stuck in her garter.

He suspected the version of Marie now before him was the tutored convent girl, her legs tucked up on the seat's edge as she sat canted on one hip. Her long braid hung over one breast. With her free hand, she toyed with the curled end. In his mind, he unbraided the plait and spread the silky cascade over a pillow. He pressed his nose into its scent.

Suddenly, she stopped reading.

"It's the end of a chapter." She looked up with hesitation. "Do you want me to go on?"

He hadn't absorbed a word she'd said, but he knew the cadence of her voice would haunt his dreams.

"No." He stood up and rounded the chair to put something solid between them. "I stoked the fire in the barn stove. It should be warm now, so I'll be off—"

"Lucas?"

Like a gulp of hot brandy, the sound of his name on her lips.

She said, "I've been thinking."

Not as much as I have.

"By the sound of that wind," she said, "I assume there's another storm coming?"

"There's always another storm coming." On the way back to the cabin, he'd watched a dark belly of clouds shadow the western sky. If his instincts were right, this storm would last for days.

"Then perhaps," she ventured, "you should sleep in the cabin tonight."

He tightened his grip on the back of his chair. A rivet dug into his palm, but not so painfully that he could forget about the bed in the other room, the sea of furs, an image of Marie sprawled among them, her arms upraised—

No.

She was just scared, thinking of the opossum.

"I fixed the door," he said. "It won't fly open. Wild things won't get in."

Her lashes made crescent shadows on her cheeks. "It isn't right for you to be sleeping in the barn. Not when there's a perfectly good bed for you in the other room."

He grunted, trying to block off the fantasy of Marie curled up with the firelight dancing on her naked skin. She wasn't offering herself up as a bedmate.

Was she?

The thought raised a lot more than his hopes

"You're asking me," he said, the air going thin in his lungs, "to sleep in this cabin with you."

"I can sleep right here." Her voice rose an octave as she slipped a leg out from under her and tapped the hearthstone with a toe. "On a pallet, right by this fire—"

"I won't make my wife sleep on the floor." He clenched his jaw. "What kind of man do you think I am?"

"I think you're a man of your word." She fussed with the corners of the pages, her chin rising. "I think you're kind, Lucas. Though...I haven't shown much gratitude for your kindness."

Hell, it wasn't gratitude that he wanted. And it wasn't kindness that pushed his blood south. Did she have any idea how hard she was tempting him now? She was just a few feet away, curled up like a cat, talking about beds. How easy it would be to lift her up, burrow his face against that lovely throat, and show her what pleasures they could share.

He checked himself.

I won't be a monster.

She said, shifting her gaze to the flames, "Have I told you the story about the house that stood just inside the walls of my old orphanage?"

"No." Another story would kill him. "Tell me about it some other night—"

"It was the caretaker's house," she interrupted, plowing forward, "but no one had lived there for a long time. A previous caretaker had died in some horrible way...or that was the rumor, anyway. I spent a night there on a dare. Boards creaking, the wind howling. And now, every time I close my eyes in this cabin"—she raised her lashes—"it feels like I'm alone, surrounded by ghosts."

For the second time in a day, he lost the capacity to move. Her midnight-blue eyes pleaded with him. He lifted his eyes to the ceiling, distracting himself by counting the knots on the pine boards. Marie didn't know what she was asking of him. There was more than one reason why he shouldn't sleep close to her.

And yet.

"You take the bedroom," he heard himself saying. "I'll sleep here."

The fire Lucas laid in the bedroom hearth had already burned the chill from the room by the time Marie bolted the door behind her. Bracing herself, she turned and faced the enormous bed she'd been avoiding since her arrival. It was Lucas's bed, so how could she not imagine him stretched upon it, stripped of fringe and breeches? In her mind, his broad chest bore a dusting of hair that caught the glint of firelight. Her palm tingled as she thought of running it over the swells of his body.

She released a deep sigh and leaned against the door. Time to stop lying to herself. She had tried to ignore this attraction, but if she were honest, she'd been roused from the first moment she'd seen him in Madame

Bourdon's salon. And now, having pressed against his solid chest, having bathed in his big body's warmth as he taught her to shoot, having felt his subtle perusal as she read...she could no longer ignore what was happening to her. She wanted to throw herself at Lucas. Not solely because she was in a dangerous place and he made her feel safe. She *wouldn't* be safe in his arms, because all her best intentions would shatter.

One kiss, and she'd be wild again.

She yanked on her bodice strings, thinking about how the nuns used to talk about the treacherous demands of the body in a way that bore no resemblance to the storm of unsettling, heart-pounding feelings that blasted away a woman's better judgment. She hadn't been alone with Lucas for more than a few days, and already she was losing her senses. But she'd be a fool to succumb.

A woman was helpless once she gave herself over to a man.

Shivering in her shift and stockings, she slid a knee onto the bed and burrowed under the thick pile of furs. She lay back, huffing out a breath, worn down by the conflicts between them and within herself. The pillow she seized smelled of feathers and cold. Lucas had told her he'd visited this cabin many times before Talon had actually signed it over to him, to walk the land and make preparations for winter. She wondered: had he brought a woman into this bed? Did he pull her naked body against his? Did he kiss the hollow behind her ear? Did that woman slip her fingers down his abdomen to take him in her hand—

Arrrgh!

She seized a second pillow and covered her head. She tossed and turned as her body's warmth took the chill out of the bed linens. The fire in the hearth leapt and popped. She squeezed her eyes shut to count backward from one hundred, as Cecile had once taught her when she first had trouble sleeping in the restless dorm. She sank deeper into the mattress as she repeated the exercise in Latin...

Marie jerked awake with a start. She opened her eyes, wondering if she'd even slept. The room was dim and red, lit by the glow of wood coals. All was quiet, but it felt more like the absence of noise, like she'd been jolted awake by some racket that still vibrated soundlessly in the air. Another restless dream, she thought, as moments slid by. She laid her head back down upon the pillow, sinking into the warmth and comfort—

And heard it again. She hauled herself up on her elbows. In the other room, something fell with a clatter.

Kicking off the furs, she seized a poker from the stand before unbolting and throwing open the bedroom door. The first thing she noticed was that the front door wasn't swinging open to the storm. The next thing she saw was Lucas, silhouetted against the hearth light, reared up to his full brawny height. His linen shirt hung from one shoulder and exposed a bare arm and the muscled nakedness of his chest. Flexing her grip over the iron poker, she searched for the danger that had put him in such high alert, but nothing else moved in the room but his bellowing chest.

"Lucas?"

At the sound of her voice, he swung a fist hard through the air. She gasped as he lost his balance, falling back against the mantel, only to keel forward again to hit the hearth chair with his knees. With a growl, he seized the chair and shoved it away, shouting something in a language she didn't recognize as he tripped and fell hard to one knee.

She pressed a hand against her throat to dull the pulse that pounded beneath. No creature of fang and claw stalked the room this time. Yet she recognized the threat all too well. Lucas was caught in a nightmare, swinging at phantoms.

Moving slowly so as not to startle him, she set the poker aside. She couldn't see his expression, not with the light behind him. His long, sun-lightened hair had come out of its rawhide tie. It lay wild about his heaving shoulders. His stance said he was ready to pounce on something, the swell of his muscles beaded with perspiration, his stomach compressed to hard ripples. The muscles in his legs bulged as he lumbered to his feet and took a staggering step in her direction.

"Lucas." She made her voice commanding, a superior officer speaking an order. "Wake *up*."

CHAPTER TWELVE

The enemy's voice rang in his head. Lucas pulled at his chest, seeking the strap of his rifle, catching nothing but cloth. His attention fixed on a faint glow in the distance, on the silhouette within. A pulse pounded in his temple as the figure moved. He reached over his shoulder to seize the bore of his rifle, only to grasp air.

"How am I to sleep, Captain, when you're raising such a clatter?"

That voice again. High-pitched, but not a war cry. Someone pretending to be an officer, a ruse to lure them all into death—

"Keep this up," said the voice, "and you'll destroy what little furniture we have."

He jerked back a step. The enemy had shortened the space between them. How had he not noticed? He'd lost too much blood, his senses were hazy. His flintlock was gone, where was his sword? He slapped his hip in search of the hilt as he saw a slim, small figure emerge from the gloom.

"I won't leave crockery on the table overnight anymore." The woman—*a woman?*—stopped just out of reach of sword, bayonet, fist. "Do you rise up like this every night, Lucas?"

The words garbled in his head. She wasn't speaking the Flanders dialect. Or Huron. *French.* She was speaking French.

Not an enemy.

He blinked hard. Saw a dark braid, a pale face against the backdrop of the soldiers grappling in the shadows.

Marie.

Why was she here? She'd be massacred on this battlefield.

Run. He tried to shout, but no words left his throat. He stepped toward her. His foot didn't sink into mud. The air didn't stink of cannon fire. The screams of horses didn't rend the air.

He paused and patted his chest, side, and arm.

He wasn't wounded.

"Are you awake yet?" Her pale face loomed close. "Help me pick up this chair, would you?"

She gestured to something on the ground between them. A mossy boulder reformed before his eyes. He slapped a hand on it. His fingers sank into the soft surface. He hauled it up with one hand. *Green brocade, stuffed with hay.* He set the thing to rights on the flat surface— *a floor*—and then fixed his attention on Marie's face—the pink mark that creased her cheek, the worry in her eyes—a rope against the pull of his delirium.

I am dreaming, he thought.

She sees me.

He jerked away, turned to the fire and flattened his hand on the mantel. The bloody tentacles of his nightmare retreated under a wave of shame. He squeezed his eyes shut.

He wasn't fit to live with a woman.

He wasn't fit to live with anyone.

Marie moved like a haunt, materializing beside him. "What was that language you spoke, Lucas?"

He bellowed air like he'd run a hundred miles, but Marie acted as calm as rain.

"You were mumbling," she continued. "It sounded...different."

"Flemish." He'd sailed thousands of miles away, but in his nightmares he still found himself on the fields of Flanders. "Or maybe Huron. I speak them both."

Have nightmares in both.

"Huron," she said, testing the name. "Isn't that one of the local tribes?"

He nodded. How could she pretend nothing had happened? Why didn't she go away, let him catch his breath?

"When I was at Etta's, before our wedding, Philippe welcomed two local trading partners. They smoked a long pipe in the study and spoke in a language I'd never heard before—"

"Abenaki." The word rasped across his throat. "Philippe speaks Abenaki. It's different."

He slid a glance toward the door of the cabin. In the barn, there wasn't any crockery to break, no woman to probe his weaknesses, and no one to see his shame.

She said, "In my father's nightmares, he spoke Spanish."

He turned his head sharply, caught a whiff of rosewater scent.

"So many times, I woke him from nightmares." She shrugged and hugged her arms. "He fought against the Spanish in the Battle of Rocroi. Have you heard of it?"

He shook his head as he fell into her eyes.

"It was a victory against the Spanish, but a disaster for my father's squadron of cavalry. On bad nights, he relived it."

He shoved away from the mantel. What witchery was this? Was this still part of the dream? He didn't feel himself yet. The madness wasn't gone, though his hands had stopped shaking, and his heart was no longer a trapped rat fighting tooth and claw. She should be bolting herself behind a door, having seen what violence he was capable of. He was more dangerous to her in this moment, as the sea of memory had receded like a tide, leaving a sucking, empty hollow—

"How my father would rage," she whispered. "My heart broke for him every time."

"I'll sleep in the barn."

"No." Her cool hand lit on his arm. "Stay here."

He breathed deep, willing patience.

She said, "We can move the chairs, and maybe the table, too. You'll cause less damage to them, and yourself." She squeezed his forearm. "I don't want to be alone, Lucas. I need you here in the cabin."

A rumble caught in his throat. She shouldn't say things like that. Did she know what her eyes promised? The oblivion of pleasure, the kind that could be found in a bottle of rum, or in the arms of a willing woman…like the one blinking up at him with the softest look on her face.

His reason fled to the shadows.

He seized the back of her head and brought her lips to his.

CHAPTER THIRTEEN

Lucas's warm mouth slid over hers with shocking wet ease.

She slapped her hands against the wall of his chest. She meant to push, but his skin pulsed against her palms. He made a rumbling sound in his throat, and immense muscles shifted under her touch. Even in the white brightness of her surprise, she knew what she should do—what she *had* to do—but her body had other ideas. Her blood thrummed like the hum of a thousand bees.

She couldn't push him away.

Her lashes drifted closed as strong, wicked currents tugged her deeper into sensation, rousing her darker angel from a long slumber. She raised up on her toes, moving her mouth against his because his rough lips felt like heaven, as did the brush of his beard against her cheek. His fingers tightened on the back of her head, holding her fixed, and a dangerous thought streaked across her mind.

Why fight what I want?

Her pulse leapt at the possibilities as his rough hand swept up her side. No shawl impeded his grasp as he gathered up the folds of cambric. She'd left her shawl in the bedroom in her haste. She'd stepped out into his presence wearing nothing but a shift. She may as well be naked, the fabric was so thin. When his roaming fingers skimmed past the side swell of her breast, the touch jolted through her like liquid lightning, sizzling away the last tendrils of sober thought.

His lips separated from hers with a sweet, wet sound. With a moan, she surged up to recapture the kiss. *Don't stop, Lucas.* Her thighs felt buttery weak. A familiar, swollen sensation throbbed in the juncture between them. Scattered thoughts careened as their lips brushed faintly once, and then again, her breath ragged, blood pounding in her ears. They were man and woman—husband and wife—brought together precisely for this joining, for the comfort that could be found in each other's arms. She ached for the tenderness of a man's touch, the comfort of an embrace, and all the promises of a hungry kiss.

Lucas lifted his face again, this time too far away for her to reach even when she stretched to the very tips of her toes. Dazed by feeling, she blinked her heavy lids open to a man of a wild and breathtaking beauty. A shock of hair fell across his brow, shading his probing eyes. How smoky those eyes, how intense he looked right now, standing in questioning suspension.

I want this, too, Lucas.

The words danced at the tip of her tongue. If he would only growl like he had before, or if he would lower his head so she could take that full lower lip between her teeth and show him how much she wanted him to keep touching her. She quivered, but the longer he delayed moving, the further the words burrowed in her throat. *Please, Lucas.* She didn't want to think, and she especially didn't want to stop. A bed waited for them in the other room.

This coupling was inevitable.

She had feared it—and ached for it—maybe from the start.

"Go, Marie."

She startled at his voice, though he'd spoken in a whisper.

"Go," he repeated, tilting his head toward the bedroom. "And bolt that door behind you."

He unshackled his grip on her head. She dropped hard to her heels. His body withdrew from her, taking all the warmth with him. She watched, bewildered, as he turned on one heel and walked with shoulders of stone toward the front door. He shoved his feet into his boots and didn't glance back as he passed into the biting cold. He slammed the door shut behind him.

Come back.

She strained her ears for his footfall.

Come back, Lucas.

Frustrated sensation churned inside her, pleasure spoiling into a pulsating ache. Had she dreamed what had just happened? Had she imagined the hunger of his touch, the wanting flickering in his eyes? She lifted her hands and stared at palms that still tingled from the feel of his warm skin. The imprint of his thumb throbbed where he'd brushed the side of her breast. She ran her fingers across lips so swollen, they felt bruised.

Strange thoughts crept around the fog of her disorientation, growing into filmy tendrils of confusion...and shame. Could it be that he didn't want her? That she'd only imagined all the signs of his interest? And yet she'd fallen into him. She'd melted against him. Now she sank to the floor, the hearthstone hard against her knees. She'd *encouraged* Lucas's kiss, *begged* for his caresses. Had Lucas not left the cabin, she would have given herself over. She would have followed Lucas to the bedroom like a lamb.

No.

She wouldn't have followed Lucas to the bedroom.

She would have led.

CHAPTER FOURTEEN

The next morning, Lucas winced against blinding sunlight as the barn door swung open.

"There you are," she said. "Not sleeping."

He squinted at her silhouette. He knew it was Marie—who else could it be?—but he didn't think she would have the grit to come knocking so soon after the lip-grappling they'd shared the night before.

"I brought you sagamité." She closed the door behind her and plunged them into softer light. "It's stone-cold now, but that's your fault for not coming to the cabin for breakfast."

She clutched the bowl in two hands, her hair pulled back so tight not a single strand came loose. So different from last night, when soft, dark wisps had flown around her passion-dazed face. He grunted and turned his attention back to the snowshoe frame lying across his lap, where he tied another strip of rawhide webbing. Futile to think about how he'd kiss her again in a minute—hell, he'd kiss her *right now*—if she wasn't glaring at him like a porcupine with its quills up.

"Leave the bowl there." He gestured to a crate with a half-empty bottle of rum atop it. "I'll eat later."

"It'll freeze if you wait." With a rustle of petticoats, she set the bowl down. "Do you plan to starve yourself?"

Of you, yes. He nudged an oilcloth lying open by his foot, revealing dark strips of meat. "I've got pemmican."

"Pemmican?"

"Dried meat. I spent last summer putting it up for times like these."

"Times when you wake up from a nightmare and then forget your promise of celibacy?"

He met those blue eyes with a slow burn in his own. He'd had the whole restless night to rue how she'd caught him in the midst of delirium, and how in his weakness he'd stolen that damnable kiss. He sure as hell didn't want to talk about either.

But he would set her straight on one crucial matter. "I didn't break a promise, Marie."

"Only just."

"Not even close, woman."

"One kiss," she said, her throat flexing, "often leads to another. A second or third kiss leads to—"

"The way I remember it, I was the one who started the kissing." He yanked another strip of rawhide through the white birch frame. "And I was the one who stopped it, too."

She made a choked sound, followed by a catch of breath. Her head swiveled on that lovely neck until he couldn't see any part of her face but the curve of a cold-kissed cheek. She wanted to deny it—he could see that clearly enough—but she swallowed the lie. It struck him like a hammer—she knew he was right.

By the saints. A rush of blood pounded in his ears. So he hadn't imagined how pliant she'd been in his arms. He hadn't imagined the moan she'd made against his mouth. Heat settled low in his belly, a warmth that had nothing to do with the fire blasting in the nearby brazier. It was one thing for him to want her—what man wouldn't want her? It was another thing to suspect *she* wanted *him*.

Shoving the frame off his lap, he shot up off the chair, making her flinch. Good. He wanted her to flinch. He wanted her to see how much bigger he was, how easy it would be for him to overpower her if he were a different kind of man. Better she see him as an ogre. Once she saw him as a bedmate, his will would be tested to the breaking point.

"Got something else to say, Marie?" He had to get her out of here before he started thinking with his breeches. "Or did you come into the beast's lair just to give me a tongue-lashing?"

"I see one stool, Lucas." Her voice was lake-ice steady. "Is there another?"

"No."

"Then I'll just sit here on the crate." Her skirts made that rustling noise as she pushed the bowl and the bottle of rum aside. "You can sit back down on that stool and stop looming over me now."

"Go back to the cabin," he warned her, "and leave a man be."

"For the next five months?"

Yes.

Damn it.

"Lucas." She drew herself up like the nun who used to slap his hand with a switch when he failed at his letters. "After last night's nightmare, I finally understand why you didn't want to marry anyone—"

"You should have bolted yourself in the bedroom." He wasn't going to admit to anything, and he didn't need her digging into his mind. "Stay far away from me when I'm in that state. I've broken men's bones in my sleep, thinking they were enemy soldiers. You could have been hurt."

"Perhaps so, if I hadn't known to wake you up first." She leaned forward. "I've seen this kind of madness before. I know how to manage it. It's a condition, not a weakness."

You're my weakness.

"Tell me the truth," she said. "You were on a battlefield in Flanders last night, weren't you?"

He eyed her in a way that had once made new recruits tremble. If she thought he was going to talk about the nightmares that made him tear his clothes in his sleep, she had another think coming.

"Don't tell me, then," she retorted. "I suppose it doesn't really matter. We both have secrets."

Philippe's warning flashed through his mind.

She's hurt in the heart.

"Here's the situation," she persisted. "Considering your condition, as well as your promise to ship me back to Paris in the spring—"

In his mind, he counted five months as twenty weeks, as one hundred and forty days, all spent in the presence of this soft-looking, frank-speaking, rosewater-scented woman who moaned in pleasure under his kiss.

"—It seems prudent to have a frank discussion about how we're going to manage a proper distance between us through the whole winter."

"I already told you. I'll stay here. You'll go back to that cabin, and leave a man be."

She cast him a baleful look. "Please sit down. I'm getting a pain in my neck from looking up at you."

He breathed deep to take the edge off his frustration. She'd taken root on that damn crate, sitting as straight-backed and proper as if she were at a king's table. He supposed she wasn't going to leave him in peace until she had her say. He sat himself on the wobbly old milking stool and planted his hands on his knees.

Her blue gaze faltered. "The winter is going to be long."

Longer than you know.

"We need to make rules." A stripe of light rippled across the curve of her cheek as she leaned back. "There should be no misunderstanding between us. We need…boundaries."

"I'll sleep here," he said. "You'll sleep in the cabin."

"That isn't necessary. The bolt on the bedroom door is strong."

She dropped her gaze. A faint flush colored her cheeks. He imagined her testing that bedroom bolt after he left, rattling it, her rabbit's heart pounding. She knew he could shatter that door with one good kick. Did she know his head still echoed with the sound of her moaning?

"I'll sleep here," he repeated, louder than he needed to.

She sighed hard. "I suppose," she said, glancing around, "you're used to living like a soldier on the march."

He glanced around the barn, seeing it through her eyes. The dirt floor, scattered crates, collection of tools hanging on the wall. A rusty bucket of water sat next to another crate that held his straight razor and mirror, neither of which he'd made much use of lately. A clean pair of small clothes dangled on a peg. A dirty pair hung drying.

Hell, he hadn't invited her in.

"If you insist on this, then I'll bring some furs from the cabin bedroom," she said into the stretching silence. "Is there anything else you would like?"

Peace. Solitude.

You.

"I'll take your silence as a no. Now it's my turn." She shifted her position on the crate, moving that plump, lovely bottom in ways he didn't want to think about. "Since we're to sleep in different buildings, I would prefer you knock before you come into the cabin."

Irritation skittered through him. "You're going to force me to knock on the door of my own home?"

"You tend to burst in without warning. I need some privacy. We are husband and wife in name only."

Not for long, if he didn't stop thinking about his rolled-up pallet within arm's reach and her spread naked upon it.

"I'll expect you for meals, of course," she added. "I won't neglect my duties, as few as they are and as badly as I fulfill them."

Three meals a day might be too much temptation, but a man couldn't live forever on pemmican.

"Also, Lucas, I'm not used to idleness. Though I didn't have many chores in the orphanage, we were always busy, and I was never alone. The nights here are long, and without female company, I need something to occupy my mind as well as my hands, besides reading."

He imagined exactly what she could do with those hands.

"Perhaps you can teach me how to do that." She pointed to the snowshoe he'd pulled back onto his lap.

He shifted it to block her view of his crotch.

"I should be able to make one of those," she continued. "I need a pair of snowshoes for myself. As it is, I sink to my knees in the drifts every time I fetch water from the river or meat from the storehouse."

He said through an iron jaw, "I'll find some birch staves and bend them to your size."

"You'll teach me?"

"It'll take some weeks. When the frame is ready, and I've got enough strips of moose hide, I'll show you how to weave them."

"Good." She tugged on the end of her shawl. "Another thought."

God save him.

"If our situation…becomes unbearable." She huffed out a little breath. "Perhaps you could go away for a day or two. For a hunt."

"I can't leave you alone."

She straightened her back. "I can manage for a few days."

"A tree could fall on the cabin. A bear could change dens and burrow under the porch—"

"It was just a suggestion. No reason to scare me."

Scaring her might be the only way to keep her safe, and him sane.

"Then since your occasional absence doesn't seem to be an option," she continued, "what can I do to make our situation easier?"

Wash your hair with melted snow so it doesn't smell of a Normandy spring. Muffle the sound of your skirts as you walk so I won't dream of your body beneath. Avert your eyes so I won't imagine you looking at me while you lie on my bed. Refrain from speaking, for every word that falls from your lips makes me want to kiss them—

"I can't hear a word, Lucas. Though it seems from your expression that you've got quite a lot to say."

He slapped his knees and shot up. "We're done here."

She gathered her skirts and took her time standing up. He kept his gaze on the wall as she walked toward the barn door.

"One more thing," she said, pausing. "If you wish, I could still read to you at night."

By the saints...did she expect him to sit there, idling, while she looked fetching in the light of the fire, toying with the end of her braid?

"The stories might hold off your nightmares. It used to work for my father." She cast a gaze toward the crate she'd abandoned, and the bottle atop it. "It's a better choice than rum."

Hell. "No need for reading."

"You're going to deny me the one useful thing I can do?"

I can think of another, wife.

"Finished talking about rules, Marie?"

"I suppose."

"Good." He sat down and seized the half-mended snowshoe. "Go back to your privacy, then. I've got work to do."

CHAPTER FIFTEEN

Marie scraped a broom over the porch, pushing powdery snow onto the drifts around the cabin. No matter how many times she swept the boards clean, she always came outside to find a glittering new layer. This was fool's work, and she didn't need any more proof she was a fool.

With a huff, she set the bristles on the porch, wrapped her hands over the top of the handle, and planted her chin on her knuckles. In the five weeks since Lucas had kissed her senseless, winter had closed around the land like a fist. The boughs of the pines that surrounded the clearing hung, weighed down by snow. Her breath was the same frosty color as the ever-cloudy sky. When she inhaled too deep, her chest ached with the chill. The air bit her face numb if she lingered too long outside. She'd made it a game, of sorts, to stand here during the short hours of slate-blue daylight to see how long she could withstand the cold, the silence, and the weight of the place.

Eyeing the spot of white sun so low in the sky, she figured Lucas would return to the cabin within an hour or so. Since their agreement, she saw her winter husband for only a few moments at breakfast, a little longer at lunch, and a fraction of the time at dinner. Every night, he brushed away her coolly extended offers to read to him. Every hour in-between, she remained alone. She, who'd once shared a dormitory with nineteen other girls, taken lessons in embroidery in a parlor full of chatter, and daily walked about the grounds in the company of her friends. She'd already read half the books on the bookshelf in the cabin bedroom. She was trying to translate the Greek in one of the older tomes. She had little else to do while waiting for Lucas to lumber into her presence in all his burly handsomeness, smelling of fresh-cut wood and frost, bringing the winter inside with him. He spoke volumes in the way he avoided her gaze. He barely offered up more than a phrase or two. Sometimes, she counted the number of words he spoke, rejoicing when the total reached twenty. After meals, he would shoot from his chair to head to the barn, his spine as stiff as iron. At this rate, half the trees on this land would be split into quarter-round logs by spring, and she'd be babbling to the rafters.

Her throat narrowed with the threat of tears. Once in a while, during those brief moments in Lucas's presence, she would catch his smoky gaze. That buzzing moment of connection always made her chest tighten. Anything could happen, if only one of them would say something, do something. How pitiful a creature she'd become, to spend each day living for a single moment.

And here it was again, the creeping desperation. Who did she have to blame for these silly thoughts and thwarted expectations? She could hardly blame Lucas. She'd made the rules. All those weeks ago, she'd had no inkling of how the isolation would stretch her as thin as a deer hide in a frame. She wasn't sure she could bear to stay here any longer—but neither could she leave.

Beyond the fog of her freezing breath, her gaze fell upon the icicles that grew down from the eaves of the porch. If they grew much thicker, they'd be like bars in a cage. The thought sent a shivering jolt of panic through her. Lifting the broom, she swung it high, whacking at the icicles until they broke free and exploded on the porch. She kept swinging until she'd loosened every one of them, shattering the silence.

Weaving amid a pile of glittering shards, she breathed hard and realized the rules just weren't working.

She wanted…she wanted…

Lucas.

She set the broom aside and dropped into the porch chair. Tears pinched her eyes. She missed the smell of pine that surrounded him, a fragrant cloud that followed him out. She missed his warmth, the way he filled up the room, how his brow lowered when he was thinking hard. She missed seeing the fold of deerskin that stretched between shoulder and hip when he twisted to hang his coat on the peg behind the door. She missed his kindness.

She wanted so much more than his kiss.

Dangerous thoughts rushed through her mind—wild, impossible paths to escape, and even riskier ideas about staying. How much longer could she endure this loneliness? What harm would there be in reaching for small comforts? The happiness she'd once hoped for was forever out of reach...but would it be so wrong to fill this emptiness in another way, in the way they both wanted?

She squeezed her eyes shut, but as her head lolled forward, a tear slipped through. It fell upon her wrist where the glove didn't quite meet the sleeve. Spring seemed like years away. Paris, a million miles farther. Another tear slid hot down her cold-numbed cheek to drip off her chin.

A creak of a floorboard startled her. She glanced up to find Lucas stepping onto the porch.

Lucas took in the sight of Marie's tear-streaked face as his heart came to a stop. He searched for blood, bruises, broken bones. Her skin was flushed from cold, her clothes unrumpled, but he saw no pain but that which shimmered in her eyes.

He spoke the obvious. "You're crying."

"It's nothing."

She swiped at her cheeks. Any fool could see she was lying. The stony face he'd crashed into every day had shattered. He stepped toward her and bent a knee to coax her gaze back to him, but, damn it, he was still wearing snowshoes. They arced out beyond the toes of his boots, complicating his effort to kneel. His hands were full, too. One gripped a flintlock, the other held the new snowshoe frames he'd spent weeks cutting, seasoning, and steaming into shape for her small feet.

Marie raised herself out of the chair. "I'll get your supper."

She stepped into the cabin before he could drop his burdens and lay a palm against her cheek. That was probably for the best. Touching her would be dangerous. Sagging into the chair himself, he set the flintlock and frames across his lap and picked at the frozen rawhide knots of his snowshoes. Had he done something to make her cry? Said something? He doubted it. He'd fought hard to follow her rules, by talking little and seeing her even less. Kicking his ice-caked snowshoes aside, he stepped inside the cabin, where she darted about like a startled bird, all winged elbows and swift turns, unnerving him even more.

"Those snowshoe frames," she said, setting pewter spoons on the table. "Are those for me?"

He nodded and propped them against the wall, along with the flintlock.

"Where are the rawhide strips?" She carried two bowls to the table. "I can't string the frames without them."

"I'll get them later." He sat on the bench and yanked off his ice-encrusted boots. "The snowshoes aren't important right now."

"They are to me." She tightened her jaw, but her chin trembled. "With snowshoes, I can leave this cabin without wading up to my waist in drifts. I can explore beyond the shoveled paths—"

"Marie." He set the boots aside. "Stop."

He stood up from the bench and approached the table, easing his weight upon a chair before swigging a cup of water he wished was rum. She stood frozen in place, eyes wide, tugging on her silver wedding ring.

"Sit." He turned the cup on the table in pointless circles. "Speak to me."

She lowered her chin. Her brows pinched together.

He sighed. "Marie, if I've done something—"

"You haven't done anything." She huffed a breath. "You have done exactly what you've promised me, good man that you are."

The words rang clear, but his mind rejected them. She wouldn't be calling him a good man if she knew the carnal things he'd been doing to her body, in his mind, in the darkness of the barn.

"These tears are my fault." She exhaled until she had no more breath. "I didn't think about the consequences of our agreement when we made it all those weeks ago. I'm not like you. I don't like being alone."

He ducked his head, frowning. He didn't like solitude either, but he couldn't blame her for thinking he did. She didn't know him before, back in France, when he'd become a soldier for the camaraderie. She didn't know, after the last battle in Flanders, how many nights he'd staved off loneliness by drinking, or in the arms of willing women. Hell, even when he shipped to Quebec with the last few soldiers he had left, he still found himself drawn to the campfires, feeling a growing affinity with the Huron braves telling tales about warrior chiefs and star maidens. It wasn't until the Mohawk campaign when everything changed, when he realized it was best he stay alone, for everyone's sake.

He turned the cup between his hands, seeing on the surface of the water the faces of so many lost companions.

"You're sad," he ventured, "because you miss your friends."

"Yes. Yes, I miss Cecile especially." She plucked at the folds of her skirts. "But it's more than that. With all this silence between us, I feel like I'm at the bottom of a deep well. I miss…I miss your company."

No. He didn't believe that. Her lovely face was easier to read in its vulnerability, but she didn't really miss *him.* The long nights and darkness were affecting her. He'd seen this sort of melancholy during the years he'd spent in a wilderness fort. More than one tough soldier had drifted from the fireside gatherings, slipping into gloominess. He and his men had learned to keep an eye on each other, find new ways to stay alert and busy during the long nights and gray days. But how the hell was he to amuse Marie, when it was torture to walk into this cabin every day, to gaze upon what he ached for but had sworn not to take?

"I can hardly think straight these days," she confessed, running her palms down her skirts. "I've come up with such mad ideas."

His chest tightened. "What ideas?"

"Leaving the cabin for Trois-Rivières, for one."

"We've talked about this."

"I thought if I wrapped myself in all my clothes, and the weather held steady, I could somehow cross the frozen river and walk to—"

"Marie." Was he such a monster? "The journey would kill you."

"I know." She pulled out a chair and fell into it sideways. "I saw tracks in the new snow the other day. Paws like that of a huge cat."

A bobcat. Maybe a mountain lion. He'd seen the trail, too.

"And yet," she continued, "the threat of lions didn't scare me half as much as my *other* idea." A tendon flexed in her throat. "Because my other idea involves you."

A buzzing current rippled through the air.

He braced himself. "Tell me."

She swallowed. "We'd have to modify our arrangement about keeping away from one another."

His knuckles went white around the cup. She'd set the rules. He'd accepted them. He'd battled his baser nature every day since.

"I have a good reason to ask this of you." Her voice tightened with tension. "It might help if I told you a story."

He summoned patience, emptying the whole damn well.

"My father and I lived by an orchard when I was young. We always had plenty of apples. One year, my father decided to make apple cider, so we mashed the fruit into a pulp and squeezed out the juice."

What the hell kind of story was this?

"I remember the buzzing of bees and the stickiness on my hands." She spread her own hands open, as if she could still see the stains. "Together, we strained the juice into bottles and stored them in our root cellar. I checked them every few days, because my father promised that we would see bubbles rising."

His ribs squeezed as he imagined Marie as a child peering at bottles of brown glass through drooping black curls.

"One night, my father woke up with a shout. At first, I thought it was one of his nightmares..." She swallowed the word and, frowning, buried her hands back in her lap. "But then I heard strange sounds coming from the root cellar. It sounded like gunfire, *real* gunfire. Papa grabbed his old flintlock. We flung open the root cellar door...to see corks shooting up off the bottles." She looked down at her lap, her brows high. "There were *too* many bubbles, so they all exploded."

He waited, grappling for the point.

"Don't you understand, Lucas? When something is under intense pressure...it explodes. Nothing can stop it."

The air thickened between them, like the front of an oncoming storm. Why did she always speak in riddles? It couldn't be that she thought *he* would explode, that he wouldn't be able to control himself. After all these weeks?

He said, "I'm not an animal."

"I know. I wouldn't ask this of you otherwise."

"Ask me what?"

"To relieve this discomfort between us." Her gaze wandered the room, alighting anyplace but on him. "So that we're not suddenly...overcome."

His whole body pulsed. But it shouldn't. Because she couldn't possibly be saying what his body thought she was saying.

"I'm willing to...change our arrangement." She bobbed her head in a quick little nod. "But the difficult part is up to you."

"Speak plainly, woman."

"I've been given to understand that a man can control, to some extent, if he's willing...whether he makes a woman pregnant."

His cock reacted as if it knew something he hadn't yet figured out. But she couldn't be talking about that.

"Pregnancy," she continued, "would complicate things between us and destroy our plans. Don't you agree?"

He grunted an assent, all he could manage.

"It would make an annulment impossible. Then I couldn't return to Paris, and you would be stuck with a wife. But if there's a way to avoid making a baby..."

"We're already avoiding pregnancy in the surest way."

"Yes." Her face flushed. "But—"

"What you're talking about is risky. Doesn't always work."

"I trust you to be...careful." She lifted her gaze. "Aren't there other satisfying things to avoid pregnancy...besides celibacy?"

A blinding white light burst in his mind. It pushed off rational thought and ushered in images he'd tried not to dwell on when he lay down alone on his pallet in the barn. All the ways he could take Marie's body, make her writhe underneath him. Visions of her stripping off her clothes, letting her hair down, crawling naked onto his bed, and offering up her sweet—

"Yes." His voice came out raw. He clung to a last vestige of reason. "If that's what you want."

"Oh, Lucas." She sucked her plump lower lip between her teeth. "I don't want to be alone in that bed anymore."

CHAPTER SIXTEEN

Marie caught her breath as Lucas shot off the chair.

He would seize her now. He would haul her up and carry her somewhere and press her down, on a bed, on the floor, on the table...he would tumble her to her back, hike up her skirts, and then flip open the buttons on his breeches. She doubted she'd see anything but the froth of her petticoats flying before he took her, but she wasn't frightened. The pressure between them had been building for so long. She could admit it now.

This was what her wilder nature craved.

He rounded the table in two strides and dropped to a knee before her. She breathed in the dizzying scent of pine resin and fresh-cut wood. His silver eyes darkened to smoke as he cupped her face and kissed her hard, a hungry kiss that coiled sensation tight and deep in her body. He shifted the angle of his head as he drew her lower lip between his. An odd thought fluttered through her mind as his kiss deepened.

This was no unleashed brute.

Lucas knew what he was doing.

A whimpering moan escaped her as his lips retreated, but not so far that she couldn't still feel his breath on her face. She leaned in for another kiss, but he pulled back farther, repeating that motion until she realized, with a swaying sense of disorientation, he had coaxed her into standing.

His fingers tightened on her jaw. "Are you sure?"

Yes. She couldn't manage the word. She could barely stand on her feet.

"I need to hear you say it, Marie."

Her lips tingled, but her tongue was not her own. Couldn't he see she was already lost?

She bobbed her chin and then added, in a breath, "Yes."

With a rushed exhale, he dropped his grip on her jaw and engulfed one of her hands in his. She stumbled in his wake as they passed into the bedroom, toward the bed piled with pelts. The whole room was cast in a dull red glow from the fire she'd lit hours ago, hoping he would agree to her mad proposition and finally make love to her.

Even if it wasn't *love* they were making.

He stopped beside the bed and swiveled to face her. The sheer size of him still amazed her. Burned in her mind was how he'd looked that night she'd caught him in a nightmare, the animal power of his bulging arms, massive shoulders, and rippled abdomen. All the strength he'd kept leashed in an effort to make her feel safe, to keep to their agreement. Now her bones melted at the realization nothing but deerskin and a linen shirt separated their bodies from merging.

A reedy thought fluttered through her mind that she should probably be acting shy or anxious—Lucas would expect innocence—

but no, no, that would be ridiculous. She'd already stripped herself naked in the parlor by admitting she wanted to give herself to him. Why bother pretending nerves when her whole body sang with eagerness? In a spurt of daring, she seized the front seam of her bodice and squeezed the two sides together to loosen the metal hooks from the crocheted loops. She peeled the russet wool apart to reveal her stays to the man watching her every move.

Lucas ran his finger across the bare skin of her upper chest. "This won't happen just once, Marie."

"Promise?"

She maneuvered her arms out of the sleeve holes and lifted the bodice high by one finger, letting it dangle for a moment before dropping it. His gaze darkened as he rewarded her by dipping a warm knuckle into the hollow of her cleavage. Could he feel her heart pounding? Could he see what he was doing to her?

"This," he murmured, running the back of his hand down her stays, "is coming off, too."

He tugged the knotted end of the lacing from beneath the skirt's waistband. His deft fingers worked the knot free. Then he yanked the crisscrossed lace out of the grommets, laddering up her chest with a swiftness that made her breasts swell tender. With a last wheeze of ribbon through the grommets, he pulled the lace free and dropped it to the floor. She shrugged her shoulders to rid herself of the stays, leaving only her shift to cover her nakedness. Her nipples puckered, and every brush of the tips against the cambric fabric shot little darts of pleasure through her.

Gripped by boldness, she flicked the fringe on his deerskin shirt. "I shouldn't be the only one undressing."

With firelight blazing in his eyes, he seized a fistful of deerskin at the back of his neck and hauled it off his shoulders to toss it into the shadows. He made swift work of the linen shirt underneath, leaving his torso naked above the low-slung waistband of his woolen breeches.

A solid wall of muscle rippled before her. She glimpsed a ridged scar on his side, a longer one across his chest, and a star-like pucker on one arm. Soldier's wounds, from sword and bullet. They made her giant of a husband look even more invincible, like his skin had the power to knit up around steel or lead. She flattened a hand on the ripples of his abdomen, his skin so warm, the light sprinkling of hair soft. She traced a finger in the furrow between the muscles, down to the dip of his navel where, below, the buttons of his breeches strained in her direction. Her palms ached to be filled with his sex.

Before she dared, he stepped closer to slide his hand up her side, the direction undeniable. Her lips parted as he cupped a breast.

"Do that again," he commanded.

Her senses swam as if she stood on the deck of a pitching ship. "Do...what?"

"Moan."

"I don't...moan." Her nipple tightened as he framed it between his thumb and first finger.

"Marie." He squeezed gently. "Do it again."

A moan launched out of her. He made a choked noise and pinched the tingling bud once more. She couldn't bear both his ravenous look *and* the pinpoint lightning he was coaxing through her, so she turned her face away. His soft hair brushed her cheek just as he bent his head and sucked her nipple into his hot mouth.

She whimpered as he tugged gently, making her inner muscles clench. She grasped his shoulders. Why hadn't she offered herself earlier? If she'd only known how safe she would feel in his hands...how skilled and patient his touch. She knew she would never have the gentle happiness of a lifelong, loving partner, but she could still seize from life what joy she could.

With a muffled groan, Lucas raised his head and banded an arm around her back. His other arm swept under her bottom, crumpling her skirts. Cradled aloft, she opened her eyes to see the rafters spinning as he twisted to lay her on the bed. Fur brushed against her bare back and sent new tremors of excitement through her. A lock of Lucas's hair came free of the rawhide tie and fell over his brow. A wave of tenderness washed through her as she reached up to comb her fingers through the silkiness. He dipped his head and pressed his lips against hers. Nudging her legs out from under his bulk, she dragged her knees up his sides to arch her aching center against his body.

He made a strangled noise and straightened up to plant both hands on either side of her.

"Woman," he sputtered, "if you keep doing that—"

"This?" she said, shimmying her hips against his lower abdomen.

"I'll be finished," he said, his voice strangled, "sooner than we both want."

She lifted her hips against his ridge anyway, loving the tremors of pleasure passing over his face. Catching her observance, he stretched his mouth in a wolfish smile and slid up against her with pinpoint deliberation. She gasped at the coiling friction.

"No more teasing," he warned. "At least for now."

Landing a bite-kiss on her jaw, he shoved himself off her, granting her a breathtaking view of shoulders and tapered waist. He nudged her to lie on her side so he could unhook the fastening at the back of her waistband. He rolled her flat on her back again, yanking off the skirt and petticoats, muttering, "Too damn many clothes," as he tossed them all away in a flutter of cotton and wool, leaving her in a cambric shift.

A hot flush suffused her body as he planted his big hands on her bare upper thighs and shoved up her shift. He blinded her for a moment as he wrestled the garment over her head. She fell back on her elbows, excited to finally be naked before him. Her breasts heaved. Her belly sank into a hollow. Her sex lay exposed to his hungry gaze. Only her black cotton stockings remained, held up by ribbons at mid-thigh. Her body pleased him, she could tell by the ravenous look on his face as Lucas loomed at the edge of the bed, taking in her nakedness as he fumbled with the buttons of his breeches.

She ached for more than the touch of his glance as he stripped himself down and kicked off wool and linen to release his member. She didn't know how much longer she could wait. She drew in a breath at the sight of his readiness and then gave in to a wicked urge. Spreading her knees apart, she offered him welcome.

His eyes met hers, darkened with surprise and desire. "You're a wonder."

"Don't stop now, Lucas. I can't wait any longer."

"That's what I need to hear."

He thrust his hands under her, cupped her bottom, and pulled her backside to the very edge of the bed. Stepping between her legs, he parted her knees so they hung over his elbows. The center of her sex throbbed against the heat of his big body as he settled himself into position. With the tip of his member, he kissed the entrance to her sex. Lovely, gripping spasms rippled through her.

Her elbows shook with strain. She resisted the urge to fall back on the bed. She wanted to watch Lucas's face as he entered her completely. She wanted to see his pleasure blooming, see his gruffness give way to need, know he wanted her.

How sweet it felt to be wanted, even if it was only for this.

"It might"—he frowned as he looked between them—"hurt some."

He slid inside her a fraction and she couldn't help wincing. Everything about Lucas was big. Her body strained to adjust, though she felt a warm dampness spread between her legs. He breathed hard as he stilled, his chest bellowing, his face strained with pleasure. Maybe he wouldn't notice no maidenhead barred his way.

She was counting on it.

"I'll try," he said, adding slight pressure, "to be gentle."

She expelled a breath as he pressed a little deeper, filling her sex. Her elbows gave way.

The back of her head hit the furs as she canted her hips to accommodate him. With a low, rumbling groan, he paused. His member throbbed, she felt every pulse deep inside her. She could no longer keep her eyes open.

His hands hit the bed on either side of her as he thrust his hips. She sheathed him to the root. He muttered something strained and sharp, but she was beyond understanding. His forward movement pushed her legs higher on his arms, opening her sex even more. His hips tensed against her inner thighs.

"Please," she whispered as the sweetness intensified. "Please."

He whispered in her ear, "Moan for me, Marie."

He rocked against her, and her pleasure surged. She seized his arms and dug furrows with her fingernails as he thrust, and thrust again, lifting her on a rising wave.

Then she could think no more.

CHAPTER SEVENTEEN

Lucas opened his eyes to a dim room and the sound of breathing.

He turned his head on the pillow. Marie lay with her back to him, nothing exposed above the furs but a pale shoulder and tangled braid. Breathing in the perfume of her, tinged with the scent of sex, his whole body went hot despite the chill of the early morning air. By the saints, she was a wonder. What happened to the prickly porcupine he'd brought to his cabin before the deep snows? His mind ran with so many questions.

But now—finally—he knew at least one of her secrets.

His wife was no virgin.

Jealousy flared, a sentiment shot from primitive deep. He knew he had no right to feel this way. Marie was his wife in name only. Though she had offered up her body of her own free will, he had no claim on her past, her future, or...anything but this moment. He'd be a fool to imagine she belonged to him for more than what remained of winter.

And yet...and yet...possessiveness gripped him and wouldn't let him stop speculating. He wondered if her lack of sexual innocence had anything to do with Marie's hurt, that pain Etta had perceived and Philippe had warned him about. Men could be monsters, especially to women. Such thoughts were torment to him, but he couldn't stop wondering. How did a young woman cloistered in an orphanage come into contact with a brute heartless enough to steal her innocence and then abandon her?

Then again, maybe her innocence hadn't been stolen.

Maybe she'd given herself freely.

Maybe she'd fallen in love.

Jealousy surged anew, threatening to consume him. Once again, he used his better sense to push it away. Marie wasn't *his*. Whatever had happened before Quebec, it was all in the past. Yesterday, she had offered him her body, her passion, and her trust. She'd chosen to share this bed with him. It was more than he'd ever expected. More than a man like him deserved.

He rolled to his side to cup her body close. Her hair smelled of rosewater. The scent filled his head, calming the gallop of his thoughts. Learning one of her secrets had unlocked a thousand more mysteries, but, with his body so near hers, his focus shifted to discovering the answer to one crucial unknown.

Would she give herself to him again?

The space between their bodies grew warm. He scooped up a curl lying across her cheek and slipped it behind the curve of her ear, revealing a nutmeg-colored freckle on her cheekbone. He'd never noticed that before, or the other fleck of a beauty mark perched on the tip of her shoulder. He moved a fraction closer, so her head slipped just under his chin. His cock strained between them but made an effort not to touch her with it. As much as he'd love to slide into her and gently fuck her awake, this new arrangement between them felt too fragile.

She was a woman who'd been hurt by a man.

She needed to be the one to make the choice.

Sighing in sleepy contentment, she shifted under the furs, brushing her bottom against him. His balls tightened. With one slight move forward, he could snug the length of his erection in the valley between her thighs. No sooner had the thought passed through his mind than the woman in his arms maneuvered her backside against him in just that position. His heart dropped a beat as his cock slid the length of her warm furrow.

He slid his arm across her waist and murmured, "You're awake."

Her soft laugh, muffled by the pillow, was as intoxicating as a swig of rum. He whispered her name into her hair. She answered by swaying her backside. That seemed like eager consent, so he slid his hand around her waist and down to the warm delta between her legs. She made the kind of sound that could be interpreted in any language as further encouragement. He nudged his fingers to open her sex. He circled the engorged little nub near the crest until she pressed her head back into his throat, her breath hissing between her teeth.

Wanting fogged his mind, but he kept a leash on his urges. He rolled his finger until her whole body undulated against his touch. Her rising pleasure fueled his own, straining his sex to tautness. His mouth watered at the sight of a pink nipple peeking just above the edge of the furs.

Her bottom pressed harder against him. A dangerous surge strained his sex.

Not yet.

His fingers were slick, she was ready for him, but he wanted more than just to satisfy an urge. He sucked her earlobe between his lips. He paused touching her nub only to slide his finger deeper and plunge it into her tight, wet opening. A little cry ripped from her throat. He considered replacing his finger with his tongue, to taste the salty sweetness of her and feel her body throb against his mouth. They would do that later, as they would do so many other things. Winter unfurled before him no longer an infinite stretch to be suffered, but as weeks of exploration. He would pleasure her here in this bed, and on the rug in the other room, and upon the dining table, and in the chair by the fire, against the wall by the door, holding her up by the buttocks as her body welcomed him. Maybe then he could make her happy—

Happy.

He stopped circling, struck by the thought, but she didn't give him a moment to ponder. She tilted her bottom again, this time so the tip of his cock burrowed against her swollen opening, where his finger had just been. His blood rushed, sizzling away the last measure of reason. He shifted his weight, nudging his thigh between her legs to raise one, giving him leverage and better access.

With one slow thrust, he sheathed his cock in her warmth from behind.

Mustn't lose control.

Mustn't.

He unclenched his hand, still buried in the dark curls between her legs, to resume rolling a finger around her pleasure. He thrust inside her to keep pace with her ever more labored breathing. The furs slipped away as they gently rocked, offering him a view of the sinuous indentation that defined her back. Suddenly, her sex clamped around him tight, squeezing, and he teetered on a thin edge.

"Lucas!"

He rode out her climax, on the brink of his own, his cock straining, forcing himself to *hold, hold, hold* until she stopped making those noises, until he felt the last squeeze of her fulfillment, until her body relaxed upon the linens. Only then did he pause, thrust once, twice, and then pulled himself out before his mind went blank.

Seizing her hip, he laid the length of his cock, stretched to fullness, between the shapely mounds of her backside. He threw his head back and, pressing himself snug against her warmth, surrendered to his body's demands for fulfillment. His senses reeled through a bright white place as he rode his pleasure with the scent of Marie in his nostrils. He didn't come back to himself until a muffled laugh brought his attention to the woman shifting in his grip. Marie peeked over her shoulder and smiled with cat-like satisfaction. Inside him, something slipped at the sight of that mischievous, knowing grin. Something he couldn't quite catch, like his still-heaving breath.

The moment left him suspended, mentally grappling, caught unawares.

"Lucas," she whispered, arching to glance toward her buttocks, flushed pink and glistening wet, because of him. "Would you mind...?"

He nodded and nipped her on the shoulder as he reached across the bed. On the commode table, he'd left a pile of linens he'd fetched after their first coupling last night, as she'd sunk into a deep sleep. Now he took a square and ran the cloth over her lower back to clean her up. Silence stretched between them in the intimacy of the moment, a chasm he was too sated to fill with talk.

"Look at you," she said as he finished up. "You're almost smiling. At least now I know how to stop you from scowling."

Their lovemaking had transformed her features in erotic ways. Heavy-lidded, pink of cheek, she was the image of a satisfied seductress taking a moment of leisure before the next indulgence. The thought kicked up a fresh wave of desire. He would do anything to make her stay like this, to make her happy.

There was that word again.

"Such a gentle smile, too." She rolled onto her back without a care to his view. "It makes you look almost friendly."

"Friendly?" That's all the wit he could muster within sight of her naked breasts.

"You're intimidating." She rose to an elbow. "Not just because of your size."

She was intimidating. Bold in her nudity. Holding so much power over him.

"But did you notice?" she asked. "You slept beside me all night and never woke up with a nightmare."

He froze. *By the saints.* He'd forgotten about the nightmares. A chill prickled over him that had nothing to do with the morning air. What had he been thinking? He shouldn't have slept in this room with her. Those nightmares would come back, they always came back. He couldn't be around her when they did—

"I don't like that face." Marie pushed a curl over her shoulder. "Don't you dare think of skulking away. There's no need. Last night, you slept like a stone beside me. I didn't know if sharing a bed would help hold back your nightmares, but I am sure it will be more effective than reading, and a better alternative than rum."

A rusty wire of disillusionment speared through him. "Is that why you gave yourself to me? Just to ease my nightmares?"

She lifted her eyebrows. "I think you know better."

He did. Yes…he did. The zeal of her response had been undeniable.

He couldn't think straight. She was twisting him up, this woman, talking circles around him. "I don't think I'll ever figure out your mind, *Anentaks*."

She narrowed her eyes. "*Anentaks?*"

"It means 'little porcupine' in the Huron dialect."

"Goodness. How many languages do you know? Never mind." She tilted her head. "What's a porcupine?"

"A small creature, about the size of an opossum, covered in sharp quills."

"Like a rodent?" That lovely black brow rose higher. "With spikes?"

"It'll shoot them at you if it feels threatened."

"Hah! What a terrible opinion you have of me."

"It's a compliment." At least, he'd meant it that way. "You're small, but you defend yourself with sharp words."

She traced a circle on his chest. "Have I really been that unpleasant?"

"Not when your quills are down. Underneath the quills, a porcupine is soft. The meat is sweet to the tongue."

A new smile played around her mouth. "So you're calling me a *plucked* porcupine, is that it?"

"You weren't shooting any quills last night."

"Best be careful." Her eyes danced as she slid a finger down to his navel. "I still may have a few quills left to shoot."

Her fingers found the sword scar on his lower rib and the longer one across his chest. Curiosity danced across her face as she traced them with a slow finger. Questions quivered in the air between them. Someday, he'd tell her about Flanders. Someday, he might even tell her the real reason he'd chosen to settle on this land.

But right now, he had questions of his own.

"What happened in Paris, Marie?" He grasped her roaming hand and brought it to his lips. "What devil took your innocence?"

CHAPTER EIGHTEEN

The Salpêtrière Orphanage
Paris, 1670

"Cecile, look!" Marie dropped to her cot in the orphanage dormitory and thrust a note into her best friend's hand. "He sent me another poem, tucked in a copy of *La Gazette.*"

"Again?" Cecile clicked her tongue. "It's a miracle you haven't been caught fetching newspapers from the garden gate."

"Never mind that." Marie nudged the hand that held the poem. "Read it, read it aloud to me."

Cecile bowed her pretty blonde head and unfolded the parchment. Marie closed her eyes as her friend spoke the magical words aloud.

My heart lies within these words.
I will leave them at your gate.
Marry me in Paradise tomorrow, fair lady,
Or my heart will surely break.

Marie opened her eyes into the silence that followed. Cecile had already refolded the parchment and was now pinching the edge.

"Well?" Marie's cheeks ached from smiling. "What do you think?"

Cecile shrugged. "Your François's poetry hasn't improved over the months, alas."

"He's a soldier, not a poet, and what does that matter?" She plucked the note back and waved it in the air. "He's declaring his love. He wants to marry me!"

The first day she'd laid eyes upon her darling François, she'd been shepherding a group of younger orphans through the streets of Paris to visit the king's menagerie. She'd been thrilled to be released from the convent to aid one of the older nuns as a chaperone. Following a few steps behind the girls through one of the many squares, she'd glimpsed a bold young man standing on a terrace above the door of a tavern.

As she'd passed below his balcony, he'd spoken loud enough for her to hear. "*Si belle, si innocente.*"

Startled, she'd glanced up past muscular legs, past a billowing white shirt open to a bare chest, and up farther to an inviting smile and pair of dancing black eyes. Bathing in his admiration, she'd laughed, too, but then quickly rushed away to catch up with her charges. It had been only a single, sparkling moment, but the rest of the day had seemed brighter, her heart lighter.

François had been there again on the return trip, when the young orphans were weary, and the bright day was coming to an end. He'd changed into a fine blue coat with silver braid and stood in the street, resting his gloved hand on the hilt of a sheathed sword. The man she'd glimpsed on the balcony was a musketeer, a soldier of the king's guard and thus of noble blood. Her heart had climbed into her throat when his gaze met hers.

His face lit up, as if she'd been expected.

"You dropped this earlier, Mademoiselle," he'd said, stepping into her path. He handed her a folded square of lace much finer than any she'd ever owned. Not wanting to attract the attention of the nun walking ahead, she mumbled her thanks, took the gift, and moved quickly on. Inside the lace, she felt the folded edge of a note.

Thus their secret courtship began.

"Marie, I'm uneasy about all this." Cecile stood up from the cot and wandered to the leaded window. "You don't know him, really."

"It has been six months, Ceci." They'd had this conversation before, she couldn't seem to convince her friend of the certainty of their love. "He's never touched me, not once, not even a hand through the gates." Though how she wished he would! "He's been loving and generous." What a trove of ribbons and lace she'd hidden beneath her mattress. "He's been respectful and so very kind—"

"I know, I know, I do want you to be happy." Cecile's freckle-dusted face tightened as she cast her gaze beyond the rooftops of Paris. "But I'm so scared. Are we really going through with this mad plan?"

"Yes." A thrill went through her at the audacity of it all, but Ceci was a bundle of worry. "Oh, please don't fret. Genny has planned everything perfectly."

"Wouldn't be better to ask Mother Superior again—"

"She won't change her mind. You didn't see the horror on her face when I asked to refuse the king's offer, or how appalled she was when I suggested another girl take my place." Marie pitched her voice like Mother Superior's. "'Marie-Suzanne, a boon from a king can't be given away like an old dress.'"

"Still. I can't believe we're doing this." Cecile fretted with her fingers. You're really going to sneak out, meet Genny, and switch clothes with her tonight?"

"Yes." The hours couldn't pass fast enough. "Tomorrow, Genny will board the ship swathed in my cloak, a King's Daughter in my place." Marie crossed the empty room to grasp her friend's hands. "And I'll leave the convent to meet François in Paris."

Cecile pressed Marie's hands against her chest. "Are you sure, in the deepest, *deepest* part of your heart, that this man is honest and good?"

"Yes." As sure as anything she'd ever known in the whole of her life.

"But..." Cecile choked down a sob. "But you'll be here, in Paris. And I'll be across an ocean. I'll never know..."

Marie's eyes grew damp. She'd been so caught up in the excitement of the adventure she forgot the sacrifice they were both making. Cecile wasn't really worried about François or the marriage. Cecile wasn't even worried about playing her small part in this adventure. Her friend was only thinking about the price they'd both pay for the choices they were making.

Tomorrow, they would forever go their separate ways.

"I'm being selfish," Cecile conceded, dropping Marie's hands. "I'll just miss you so much."

"I wish we could *both* escape tonight. I wish you'd fallen in love with someone in Paris, too." She embraced her friend and spoke softly in her ear. "But you won't be alone during your grand adventure, my friend. Genny will be beside you all the way. In Quebec, you'll find a husband who'll love you, I'm sure of it. Once I'm settled, I'll write."

That evening, Marie slipped away to meet Genny, and everything went as planned. Set free of the convent walls, Marie raced through the streets of the city, sharp gravel scattered under her feet as she traveled by the light of the moon. She navigated purely by memory of the route she'd taken half a year ago. Her feet hardly touched the ground until she found herself in front of the public house with the painted red stag.

The windows of the Paradise tavern were ablaze with candlelight despite the late hour. She burst through the doors, pausing as a dozen pairs of eyes fell upon her. She had a moment's hesitation. Was this really François's home between military assignments? She'd seen it only from the outside. Groups of ill-dressed men gathered around tables, quaffing wine and playing cards. Women carried platters and pitchers, sashaying among the tables in shortened skirts and low bodices. Everyone seemed to be in a very good mood.

She heard her name shouted from a corner, and the tendril of worry withered.

"Marie-Suzanne!"

François swung up from a chair, toppling it in his eagerness. His mustached face beamed. She wound around the tables to meet him halfway, where he swept her up. His lips found hers. That first kiss was better than any she'd pressed into her pillow in practice. His thin mustache tickled her, though his breath tasted of strong wine.

"*Mes amis*, my true love is here at last!" François turned to face his friends—Benoit, Julien, Yves—who applauded from their corner, bowing their heads as each was introduced. "I must end our night's revels, for my love is here! *À bientôt!*"

François hurried her up a set of stairs to a second-floor room. Dizzy with giddiness, she recognized the window, swung open to the street, and the balcony beyond, where she'd first glimpsed him all those months ago.

"My darling," he murmured, cradling her. "I knew you would brave all terrors to be with me tonight. I've wanted you at my side so badly."

He set her on the bed. She hardly had a moment to absorb the shock of where she was—in a man's lodgings!—before he started kissing her as she'd always dreamed he would, soft, gentle kisses that made her insides warm like she'd drunk a gallon of the nun's special broth. A sweet April breeze drifted over them, carrying the scent of flowers. She became aware of a tugging upon her clothes and realized his roving hands had already unhooked her skirt, unlaced her bodice, and now he was pulling everything off her body with deft hands.

"François," she gasped as she found herself wearing only a shift. "Shouldn't we wait—"

"Wait?" He gripped her cheeks and looked deep into her eyes. "Did I not make you a promise, my love?"

"Yes."

"Soon enough, we'll be bound forever." He kissed the tip of her nose, seized the hem of her shift, and slid it out from beneath her bottom. "But this love between us cannot wait another moment."

Warnings tickled her mind. The nuns would not approve, but they'd also taught her all men were sinners, and the body was weak, and forgiveness always came with God's mercy.

Though she hadn't realized how weak a body could be until François pulled away the last of her clothing.

"Ah, Marie," he gasped, "your body is art come to life."

She crossed her arms as his gaze feasted on her. In the orphanage, they didn't even *bathe* naked.

"Don't be shy, my sweet darling." He nudged her arms away. "How I've dreamed of seeing you, of touching you like this!"

François ran his hand over her breasts. Her unease was swamped by other, more powerful feelings. He stoked those feelings as he trailed his fingers down her abdomen and then sank them deep between her legs. The intimate touch made her pulse leap.

When he pulled his fingers away, she cried out in protest until she saw he'd paused just to wrestle out of his clothes. Pulling off his shirt, he revealed a lean chest sprinkled with dark hair, so curiously different from her own. He shoved down his breeches and small clothes, and his man's part leapt into view, taut and straining against his abdomen. She bit her lower lip, shocked by how reckless this was. Shocked, too, at how her woman's parts tingled in anticipation. François was right—this love *couldn't* wait. Why taint their first moment together with talk of impropriety, when they would be married for a lifetime?

With a smile and murmured words, François urged her to scoot back, lie flat on the bed, and open her legs so he could see her treasure. Her inner muscles throbbed as he climbed over her and positioned his swollen member against the place his fingers had once been.

"Ah, my sweet virgin," he whispered. "You are mine now, forever."

He thrust himself between her legs. She startled at a pinch, wincing as he pulled his sex out of her and then thrust in again.

She gripped his arms. "François, that h–"

"Wait, my love," he said, his voice strained as he continued moving. "The pain will pass in a moment, I promise."

She caught her breath at the thrusting soreness, her whole body rocking with the movement of his pumping hips. But he was right, so right, as new feelings rose, and the soreness ebbed. The pleasant anticipation she'd experienced before, when he'd first touched her with his fingers, returned with rising pleasure. Pushed by stronger and stronger ripples of sensation, she felt a moan rising to her throat. Then François suddenly shouted, arched up, and pulled his member out of her.

She stilled, not sure what was happening. François squeezed his eyes shut as if in pain, gripping his male part against her belly. Not long after, he rolled off her, breathing hard, leaving moisture by her navel. Embarrassed, she patted the mattress to find a corner of the linen sheets so she could wipe it off.

"François." She folded the linen edge away and turned toward where he lay, an arm thrown across his brow. "We're lovers now, aren't we?"

"Lovers indeed." He turned his head, black eyes twinkling under half-closed lids. "Did I make your body sing, my darling?"

She ducked to hide a smile. She'd never felt as alive as she did right now, though it came with a strange jitteriness. "So this is the pleasure of the flesh that all married people enjoy?"

"Yes, but there's one difference." He flattened a hand on her belly where she'd wiped away the moisture. "Did you see how I finished outside your body?"

She nodded, though she didn't really understand. Shyness and curiosity warred within her at this frank talk.

"I did that," he said, "so I wouldn't fill your womb with child." He touched the tip of her nose. "I would not leave you in such a condition, my darling."

"Not until we're married," she added.

"Oh, my darling, we're married as of tonight, in my mind." His grin rivaled the shining of the moon through the window. "And this is only one of many pleasures we can share with our bodies until that happy day."

"Are there others?"

"Yes." He slid down the bed, raising her knee so he could duck his head under it. "I shall teach you every single one of them, *ma belle innocente*, that I promise."

François kissed her again, but not on the lips. She arched up against the pillow at the graze of his tongue, wondering if there was anything more glorious than love.

Weeks passed by in a haze of warmth and satisfaction. She hardly left the room except to use the privy. With her body adjusting to new pleasures and heart cradled in François's affection, she dozed and napped through the days. Occasionally, he left the inn for an hour or so, but he always returned with knitted silk stockings, or ribbons she saved for her wedding bouquet, or feathers for the veil she might wear, all of which he taught her to play with in inventive ways. He encouraged her explorations, told her anything she demanded to know, and praised her eagerness to learn a wife's duties in the bedchamber. She adored the sight of his face when it squeezed with pleasure. One day, his friends banged on the door, demanding his presence downstairs for their amusement, but he shouted them off, saying he wanted only to be with his darling fiancée.

Until, one day, he didn't.

She felt like she'd been drinking from a spigot of enchantment and then it abruptly ran dry. She'd been left alone in the room for half a day when she first noticed the change in him. She'd crept downstairs to look for François, only to be warned by one of his friends to stay in the room lest she be recognized and marched back to the orphanage. When François returned hours later, his smile shifted to irritation when she again brought up the subject of finding a priest. Later, he warned her he was running out of lessons to teach her. More and more, he reeled into the room smelling of wine, enticing her to please him without bothering to please her in return. After a week of this strange transformation, she found herself awake in the nights, watching him snore out fumes, searching for the devoted man who'd made so many promises.

Cecile's misgivings drifted back to her. *Are you sure, in the deepest, deepest part of your heart, that this man is honest and good?* To think Cecile was on a ship by now with Genny and the other King's Daughters, several weeks into the Atlantic.

No. She was letting her thoughts run wild only because she was alone too much. She wasn't accustomed to solitude and indolence. She had too much time to worry and think. One day, she couldn't stand it anymore. She crept to the top of the stairs to listen to the men laughing and watch the women carrying trays through the room. She saw a woman sitting on a man's lap. She figured they must already be married, because unlike François, who kept her hidden away, this man dipped a hand into his wife's bosom for the whole world to see.

Then, amid the noise, she heard François's rolling laugh.

She flew down the stairs, ignoring the sudden attention as she raced to François's table, in the same corner where she'd found him that very first night. He sat with his three friends, the remnants of dinner on plates before them. He caught her gaze as she approached. She smiled her brightest smile.

After an odd pause, he smiled back.

"There she is, my little dove." His eyes were bloodshot and rheumy. "We were just talking about you."

The heads of the other musketeers swiveled her way. She sensed a shift of heat in the room, a curdling of air. She turned away from their ogling and focused on François, darling François, whose affections she'd somehow lost and now had to find a way to win back.

"Sit, Marie." François patted his knee, though the shine in his eyes had sharpened. "Come get to know my friends better."

She didn't care about his friends, but she did want to be closer to François. So she slid onto his lap. François seized her. He yanked her back against his chest so hard she was forced to face his amused friends, her chest thrust out.

"François," she whispered, wincing as his fingers dug deep. "You're hurting me."

"Am I?" François planted his chin on her shoulder. "A forgotten lesson, then. Someone else will have to teach you that."

Her heart stopped cold.

"These are the sweetest tits you'll find from here to Rouen, boys." François released one of her arms to slide his hand across her bodice. "Her nipples are small and tight, sweet like wild strawberries."

Her mind went white-blank. He'd drunk himself into madness, her François. She struggled in his grip as his three friends watched with gleaming eyes.

"She likes when you roll her nipples." François bobbed his thigh, making her bounce in a suggestive way. "She likes everything, this one."

"François." She tried to surge up, but he jerked her back to his lap. "Stop it."

"Ah, Marie. Those are words I've never heard you speak."

Ugly amusement rippled around the table. François's grip felt like claws. Why was he doing this to her? Why would he talk like this when he'd promised to marry her? A tremor shook through her, rattling her confidence.

"Did I forget to tell you, Marie? You're going to make me a fortune, playing the virgin. But alas, that trick won't work with my dear friends, who have other lessons to teach you." He pressed his lips against her ear. "Tell me, who among these fine soldiers would you like to take first into your sweet little body?"

Beyond the buzzing of her ears, she heard the men bartering for her. She turned her face away from the musketeers, from the table, from these strange things happening. What she saw made her eyes scald. That woman on the man's lap was not a wife. That man was not her husband. The couple climbing the stairs weren't in search of a priest. Ceci had been right to have misgivings.

François didn't love her. He never intended to marry her.

He'd been training her to be his whore.

She groped the table, seeking purchase, and instead felt the hilt of a knife under her hand. She seized it and then dug an elbow into François's ribs. Shoving off his lap, she turned and swung the weapon wide, watching his friends' leers dim at the flash of steel.

François shot up from his chair. She swung the knife in a swift and wider arc, felt the drag on the tip as the blade sliced through a layer of his musketeer's coat. François shoved his hand through the vent she'd made, outrage spreading over his face. She didn't wait to see more. She bolted for the door. Her boots pounded on the cobblestones as she fled down the street. Once around a corner, she heard the tavern door burst open and François' shouting commands. She veered down another narrow lane, then made a sharp left down another. Soldiers' boots scuffled on the cobblestones as they passed the corner and kept going. Deep in the maze of the city, she propelled herself forward, weaving from alley to street, losing herself in the labyrinth of the neighborhood, tears dripping from her face.

When sense came back to her, she headed to the one safe place she knew. Lungs burning, she flung herself against the gates of the Salpêtrière, still gripping the knife in her hand.

CHAPTER NINETEEN

What devil took your innocence?

Had Lucas swung a hammer, Marie could not be more stunned. How could he be so sure she wasn't a virgin? Could a man tell so easily? On that foolish day when she'd given herself to Francois, she'd felt nothing more than a twinge of pain. François hadn't even paused in his pleasure. The barrier seemed such a fleeting thing. Had she given her secret away somehow, by rolling in bed with Lucas like the wanton François had taught her to be?

Her heart squeezed. She knew no other way. Showing pleasure felt as natural as laughing, as weeping, as breathing. But what did she really know about what was natural, or right, or expected, between a man and woman who had any respect or affection for each other, like those who'd taken vows?

"Marie." Lucas tightened his grip on her hand, his eyes soft with concern. "You're shaking."

She thought, *No, it's the bed shuddering. It's the room itself.* Her teeth rattled against one another, jarring her gently, and she realized Lucas was right. Her whole body was trembling, from her toes to her breath. All the secrets she'd hidden so deep vied to rise to her lips.

"Men can be monsters." Lucas cupped her cheek in his hand. "Whatever happened, all blame lies with the one who hurt you."

"He was," she gasped, words filling her throat, "a terrible, monstrous man."

The story tumbled out of her, unfurling in a tangle of words. She told Lucas about the plan hatched by her and Genny and Cecile, she told him about François's empty promises and false claims of love. She turned her back to Lucas when she confessed the worst of her sordid foolishness, so ashamed of her stupidity. Francois had tucked her away from the world and made her his captive. She'd given herself away, not knowing any better. She told Lucas how cruel Francois had been when he revealed his plans for her, and how she'd seized a knife and swung it at her deceiver. She heaved as if she were still racing through the streets of Paris.

"Mother Superior took me in, when it was all over, but she had no choice but to call the authorities and report my deception." She swung her legs over the edge of the bed, remembering the suffocating stench of pomade as men in velvet coats and gold braid sneered down at her. "They accused me and Genny of hoodwinking the king. They said because of our ruse, every bachelor in Quebec would wonder whether the high-born among the King's Daughters weren't really just laundresses in disguise. And no matter how hard I insisted that I'd *gifted* the honor to Genny, they accused her of stealing the three hundred silver coins the king gave for my dowry. They called us swindlers, thieves, the worst of villains. Then they shipped me here to identify the woman who'd taken my place."

She clutched her ribs, sore from gasping. What could Lucas be thinking? She heard not a single creak of the bed-ropes, not the slightest rustle of cloth behind her. Fear stopped her from looking at him, lest all kindness be washed from his face.

"When I arrived in Quebec, Talon threatened me with such terrors. I had no choice but to identify Genny as my accomplice." She raised her chin. "But the authorities mistook me for someone helpless. They put me in a convent cell, not in a jail cell. At the first opportunity, I slipped away and set Genny free. I couldn't bear for her to pay the price of my foolishness. " Silence hummed in the room, broken only by the low crackle of the dying fire. "You know the rest."

She swiped moisture from her shame-scorched face. She felt as emptied as a sack of wheat, squeezed free of every grain. She couldn't bear to look at him, see scorn or contempt. She shoved herself off the bed.

Seizing her shift from the tangle of clothing, she struggled her arms into it, letting the hem fall below her knees to cover her utter nakedness.

The mattress creaked behind her. "Marie—"

"You must be hungry." *Don't ask me anything. Please. I have nothing left to give.* "I'll put some cornmeal into the pot and start—"

"Forget about food."

His voice was firm, unyielding. Her shoulders tightened. "You say that now, but you'll think differently when your stomach is growling and there's nothing in your bowl."

"Please stay."

Tears pricked behind her eyes. She found her corset on the floor, but not the ribbon to weave through the grommets. The urge to flee into the empty wilderness was unbearable. Right now, she'd prefer to confront a bear or a lion or one of Lucas's mystical moose rather than answer any questions or be subjected to his pity.

Or worse...disgust.

"I've always known something bad happened." His voice unnerved her in its steadiness. "Etta warned me that you'd been hurt."

Hurt. As if she'd scraped a knee or bruised an elbow. What a shock it must be to learn a different truth. She crouched down, making herself small as she pretended to search for the ribbon while wishing she could disappear between the floorboards.

"Did you love him, Marie?"

She swayed on her heels. She remembered Francois's sweetly flattering poetry, the secret notes, and the excitement of the courtship. Most of all, she remembered Francois's dancing black eyes, and the moment they turned rapier sharp.

"I believed I loved him." She glimpsed the corset ribbon and gathered it to her chest. "I wanted it to be true." Was it so terrible a dream, to yearn to be loved? "It's an old story, Lucas. He was the devil, and I was the fool."

"Stop."

The mattress creaked as Lucas stood up. He began pacing along the length of the bed.

Of course he was angry. She didn't need Francois's lessons to know a husband didn't like discovering that the woman he'd married—even in name only—had been with another man. Let him be angry, then. If this was the limit of Lucas's kindness, then it would be easier to never fall into the trap again, of mistaking joy in the bedchamber for something more profound.

She mustered some dignity and rose from her crouch. She wrapped the corset around her body, imagining it a cage around her heart, and the ribbon she wove through the grommets the lock to keep it safe.

"You're no fool, Marie." He stepped into his breeches, then approached to face her, intimidating in his shirtless beauty. "I know it, because it's taken me this long to piece you together."

"Piece me together?" She glanced at his torso, riddled with scars. "Like *you're* pieced together? You've said not a word about all of that."

"You can see my wounds, Anentaks. Until now, I couldn't see yours."

She frowned as her fingers fumbled with the laces. She was the one wearing clothes, yet she'd never felt so naked.

"I'd kill that soldier for you." He filled the air between them with his body's heat. "I'd skin him alive over burning coals for what he did."

The ends of the ribbons fluttered from her hands. He sounded angry, but not at her. He sounded protective...possessive. But no—they were words, only words. Lucas's honor was involved. His fury at Francois had nothing to do with her, not really...and yet a fluttering of a thousand wings began in her belly.

He commanded, "Look at me."

She slid her gaze up the strong column of his throat, the cut of his jaw, and the temptation of his lips. She met the storm clouds in his eyes right before he lowered his head and kissed her.

The walls dissolved around them. The floor beneath the soles of her bare feet grew warm. No draft teased the hem of her shift, or sifted up to cover her skin with goosebumps.

She was buoyed up high, like a child lifted into golden sunlight. Summer burst in her mind. Bees buzzed amid the fragrance of apple blossoms and time slowed to a trickle. She was safe in this place.

She felt...cared for.

Loved.

He pulled away and cupped her cheeks.

"That man is your past. He will never hurt you again." He tilted her face up so she couldn't avoid looking into his eyes. "And neither will I."

CHAPTER TWENTY

Hauling a burlap sack of cornmeal on his shoulder, Lucas trudged to the front of the cabin, pausing when he noticed thatch marks on the snow. The hatched pattern trailed off to the riverbank, where he glimpsed Marie stepping around the drifts, practicing in her new snowshoes.

His steps faltered, as did his heart these past weeks every time he came upon her. He carried ten kilos of weight on his shoulder, yet his feet seemed to rise from the ground. What the hell was happening to him? Since that day she'd shared both her body and pain, his world had shifted. Even the sky looked different, bluer than the tips of the spruce trees. He had a hundred tasks to finish before the coming of spring, but Marie was a distraction he couldn't resist. He slung the bag of meal off his shoulder and onto the porch, surrendering to the internal compass that urged him on a path toward his winter wife.

She gifted him a smile from beneath a fur hat. His pulse shot up. He jerked his chin to her new snowshoes. "You're walking like you're born to them."

"Confess." She narrowed her eyes against the brightness of the sun. "You tightened the rawhide weave on the left one while I was sleeping, didn't you?"

He shrugged and felt the stretch of his own grin. He'd snuck out of bed after she'd fallen asleep to finish the task. He'd also rewoven the other snowshoe so she wouldn't have to labor any longer. She'd been trying so hard, but she didn't have the strength to pull the rawhide strips tight enough.

"That's against our bargain." She tilted her head in playful scolding. "You're supposed to be teaching me wilderness skills, not doing them for me."

"It's a minor offense."

"I can hardly reprimand you." She rocked from one furry boot to another. "I have wings on my feet now. And they're so clever."

"You'll get around the place easier."

"I'm just glad I can venture beyond the porch."

He peered into the woods, wary. "Don't go too far, Anentaks."

"Worried about bears?" She shrugged. "I'll take the flintlock with me."

He let that sink in, remembering Marie in ribbons standing proper and pretty in Madame Bourdon's salon. Now she wore fur boots and breeches she'd sewn from moose hide. They clung to her lovely backside as she chattered about wielding a flintlock. He hadn't thought she could conform to wilderness life, but she was, in small degrees. Seeing her execute a second twirl in the snow, a small fraction of worry lifted from his shoulders.

"Did you just come to watch me frolic?" Her voice dropped a husky octave. "Or is there something else you need?"

I need you.

The thought shot deep. Last night had been the first calm night after a long stretch of snowstorms, and they'd honored it by cutting into the ham he'd been smoking for weeks inside the chimney. She'd entertained him by reading a lustier chapter from the tales of Pantagruel. They celebrated another way, later. After they'd satisfied each other, he'd lain awake with her curled against him, warm in her sleep, while he sought answers amid the darkness. The darkest part of winter had already flown by. With every passing day, the light lasted longer. He figured they had at least six weeks left, at best. It didn't seem long enough to get his fill of her.

He wished the situation was different.

He wished he could ask her to stay.

"I saw a stag this morning," he said, shaking off the thought. "I'm going for a hunt."

"Oh?"

"Come with me." He didn't want to waste a moment. "It'll give you a chance to use those shoes."

She wrinkled her nose. "Won't I slow you down?"

"No." *Yes.* "Stealth wins over speed in hunting."

Her face bloomed. It warmed him like a brazier.

Damn, he was lost.

An hour later, he followed deer tracks southwest into the pine woods, with Marie trailing behind. He kept to the shadows to avoid the glare of open fields, blinding this time of year with the sun so low. While Marie learned to slide her snowshoes across the surface, he crouched now and again to seek sign and scat. He'd long lost the trail of the original buck, but he discovered a new set of tracks farther along. He showed her where bark had been worn off trees from the scraping of antlers. Once, he heard her humming and didn't have the heart to shush her. He enjoyed the journey as he eyed new tracks leading toward an area where the brambles grew thick.

Too thick for them to get through without hacking.

She came up beside him, whispering, "Did we lose him?"

"He's hiding in there somewhere. He may come out the other side."

"Oh." She planted her hands on her hips, looking around, her breath a pure white cloud of mist. "Are we still on your land, Lucas?"

"I'd say yes." He resisted an urge to warm her chill-kissed face with his hands, or to kiss the little freckle on her cheekbone.

"How far does it go?"

"Miles in every direction." He wasn't sure exactly how far south they'd drifted in their westerly wandering. He'd never marked the boundaries of the landholding. He never intended to. Once you drew boundaries, men took it in their heads to cross them and churn up conflict. He didn't want this world to become the old world, where new boundary lines were painted with the blood of soldiers.

And innocents.

"So much land." She tilted her head back, closing her eyes against the blinding sky. "Such an endless forest. I have no sense of where we are."

"I'll teach you to orient by landmarks, the sun, and the horizon."

"It's so easy to get lost in this."

Exactly. "Let's take a break."

He reached out and drew her close. A knowing laugh rippled out of her, muffled against his coat of leather and fur. He led her toward a towering pine and the circle of almost-bare ground at the base of the trunk.

Swinging her up in his arms, he sank down with the bark at his back and settled her across his lap. She lay against his chest, one soft hip canted between his thighs. A sigh escaped her as she let the backs of her snowshoes sink into a drift.

Biting the end of a glove, he yanked it off and spit it onto the snow beside him. In search of the waistband of her breeches, he slid his bare hand under her coat.

"Lucas…" She adjusted her position to give him greater access. "What wicked thing do you have in mind?"

He found the belt holding up her moose-skin breeches, loosened it, and slipped his hand just beneath. The cambric of her shift bunched against his palm.

In a breathless voice, she murmured, "And I thought we were hunting a stag."

"I hunt what I can catch." He ran his lips against her temple as he gathered up folds of cambric, the moose-skin tightening across the back of his knuckles. "I just found a pretty doe."

"Are you suggesting, Captain Girard," she said, arching her back, "that you've been stalking me the whole time?"

"I can't fool you."

She looked at him through half-lidded eyes. "I feel the bore of your gun against my hip."

"It's loaded."

"Can I help you shoot it?"

"It may go off all by itself," he murmured, "if you keep talking like that."

"If it doesn't," she said, shifting her hips against him in a way that made his loins heavy, "I promise to make it go off later."

His sack tightened at the promise. She'd handled his sex more than once before, when her courses had arrived, and they'd been forced to be more creative in their shared bed. Spurred by her teasing, he maneuvered his hand a little lower under her breeches, until his bare fingers found warm flesh.

She started. "Cold! Cold."

He splayed his hand over her softly-furred mound, pausing. "Do you want me to stop?"

"Never."

The word gave him a jolt. Could there be a never? Could he always have her in his bed, keep her close, please her like this? The stunning thought hung in his mind, until she wiggled her hips and the rush of his pulse brought his attention back to the task at hand.

He murmured against her chilled cheek, "Open your legs for me, Marie."

Her thighs slackened. His fingers delved deeper. He watched her mouth part as he slipped a cold finger over the nub of her sex.

She sucked in her lower lip.

He whispered, "You're so wet."

He rolled his fingers and watched her eyes flutter closed. He explored her folds, his heart pounding as she made that moaning noise that had the power of a cannon blast on his senses. When he curled a now-warm finger deeper, her inner muscles clenched around it.

"Oh…Lucas."

Her body trembled against his. Tension tightened her limbs. He could feel it even through the layers of fur and clothes. She pressed her face to his chest as, with gentle but more insistent circles, he worked her beautiful body. Guided by her moans, he increased the rhythmic, coiled pressure of his fingers. His hand grew warm against her sex, slick with her excitement, until finally she bowed off his lap in spasms of pure pleasure.

He pressed his lips against her forehead, prolonging her pleasure with the subtle working of his hand, loving how her inner muscles unclenched in measures while her body went slack in his lap.

He cupped her hot, faintly throbbing sex, not wanting to let her go, in so many ways. He laid his head back against the trunk and watched a small cloud scud against the pale blue sky. Attuned to her breathing, he stared beyond the distant hills shimmering in the cold winter light. A profound sense of peace settled over him, sitting there with her snuggled against him, his back against an ancient tree, beneath a timeless sky.

Maybe this moment could last forever.

Maybe the danger had passed.

Maybe he *could* ask her to stay

"Lucas?"

She blinked an eye open, looking up at him through a tangle of dark hair that had slipped out from beneath her hat. The edge of that eye creased with a smile. The sight dove through the shadows in his heart to nestle like a spark.

"You forgot to fire your weapon," she murmured as he felt a pull on the buttons of his breeches. "Shall I squeeze the trigger for you?"

CHAPTER TWENTY-ONE

Her body buzzing with satisfaction, Marie followed Lucas as they worked their way around the thicket in search of the elusive stag. He glanced over his shoulder now and again to make sure she was keeping up, shooting her a roguish half-smile that only fed her wicked delight. How could she feel this giddy, stomping about in the nipping cold in the middle of these primitive woods? Yet she couldn't help herself—she pulled this cloak of happiness closer. When, eventually, she shipped back to the cloistered halls of the Salpêtrière orphanage, would she ever feel as alive as she did right now, roaming the wild with her lover?

I will miss this.

I will miss you, Lucas.

The thought came over her like a shadow. She hustled it away until the darkness retreated. She didn't want to think about the future, especially the spring, and the conversation she and Lucas would need to have then. Instead she fixed her attention on the scent of pine, the crunch of the snow beneath her snowshoes, the faint, tingling numbness of her cheeks. Most of all, set her eye on this wonderful man, striding ahead, the folds of his coat flexing across his powerful back. She would embrace this joy for exactly what it was. Never again would she confuse sexual passion for other, deeper feelings she might stupidly mistake for love.

Lucas stopped abruptly, and she followed his lead. They'd followed the tracks of the stag into a clearing. Bright, white sun glittered on the surface of the open field. Icicles hung from the boughs of the pines that rimmed it, making the edges sparkle.

Nothing moved.

She slipped up beside him. "Do you see the stag?"

He didn't nod or shake his head or even acknowledge her question. Not even the fringe of his jacket swayed. His stillness made her wary and heightened her senses. They might not be the only creatures hunting today. Patting her waist in search of the knife tucked under her belt, she waited. But the only thing she witnessed moving across the field was snow-powder kicked up by a breeze.

Under his breath, he muttered, "Damn it."

"Lucas?"

His lashes flickered as if he'd just realized she stood beside him. "We've wandered too far."

She touched the sleeve of his coat. "Then let's go back to the cabin."

His eyes narrowed in a deeper squint and a muscle flexed in his cheek. A lot of thinking was going on.

"Can't leave yet." He sighed hard. "You need to see this."

"See what?"

"Soldiers. My men."

Surprise made her pause, but Lucas shot ahead. She set off after him, but he made no effort to slow his pace. What was he seeing that she couldn't? The glancing sunlight off the snow in the open field half-blinded her. She supposed there could be campfires under the boughs of those far trees, but no smoke drifted above the treetops, and no cabins were visible between the tree trunks either. Why would Lucas's men be here, so deep in the wilderness? He'd told her many times there wasn't a soul within walking distance of their cabin.

The front edge of her snowshoe struck a broken crust of ice. Stumbling, she tipped forward but slapped a glove on the ground before her face hit powder. When she straightened, a considerable gap had stretched between them. She set her feet into the grooves of his wake and pushed harder. Her legs ached. If there were soldiers beyond those trees, she would ask Lucas if they could spend the night among them. Rest and a warm fire sounded lovely, a long walk home didn't. Besides, curiosity was getting the best of her. She wanted to meet his men and understand why Lucas was heading toward them with fierce intent.

In the blue shadows cast by the tree line, Lucas paused. He tossed his flintlock aside and shrugged off his pack. Bending over, he picked at the knots on his snowshoes, kicked them off, and then fell to his knees.

By all that was holy, what was going on?

As she came closer, it appeared by the rhythmic shift of his shoulders he was digging in the snow. By the time she reached him, he'd finished one hole and shuffled to the side to start another. He didn't lift his head when she slid up next to him, though her heaving breath couldn't possibly be easy to ignore.

The first hole revealed the top of an ice-encrusted post. Was this a boundary marker, perhaps for someone else's land? Lucas had said they'd traveled too far. Awkward on her snowshoes, she dropped to one hip so she could scrape away the powder clinging to the face of the post. She assumed there would be a bright cloth tied to it, to make it easy to see from afar.

Instead, she uncovered faded letters carved in the wood.

Henri, it said. And beneath—

R...I...P

Lucas braced himself as Marie's hazy shadow fell across the first hole. She'd be expecting an explanation, but he was still stunned to find himself in this place. Words jumbled in his mind. His tongue stuck to the top of his mouth. He didn't know what to do except keep digging. He summoned a memory of Jacques, from St. Malo, who'd joined the regiment to escape a harder life on the sea; of one-eyed Henri, who'd left behind a Huron wife and rambunctious son; of Gabriel, the pup from Perpignan, so skinny and scared his knees used to knock when he marched.

These and three others. All dead and buried.

Because of him.

"Dear heavens, Lucas, what happened?"

Why was she here? He hadn't meant to lead her here. He'd been distracted by her humming, by tracking the stag. He'd been fooled by how different the land looked when it was smothered in snow.

And yet he knew she should see this.

It was past time she knew.

"These are my men." He pointed toward the row of pale blue dimples that marked the position of the other graves. "They were the last soldiers of my regiment from Flanders."

"Flanders," she repeated softly. "From your nightmares."

His throat closed up. To think these men had survived the bloodbath of Flanders only to die so far from home.

A soft pressure brought his attention to Marie's hand on his sleeve.

"I don't understand, Lucas. Why are they buried here, and not on that battlefield across the sea?"

"These were the survivors of Flanders." Each word an iron dagger, dug deeper into his gut. "There were few of us left after the battle.

We stayed together when our company was disbanded."

She spoke softly. "So your men came here?"

He nodded. "The only thing we all knew how to do was soldier, so we sought another company. I heard of a new regiment, a Piedmont commander looking for men to come here, to Quebec." A new start in the new world, so he'd thought. No more marching in formation into a hail of lead on European fields. No more spilling blood to shift a border that would make one king richer than another. "We were told we'd guard trading posts in frontier forts."

They did, for a while, he told Marie. But within two years, he and his men were pulled from their posts and mustered into battalions to fight alongside the Huron against the Mohawk. A cursed campaign. He still could hear the mosquitoes swarming, buzzing their high whine, biting welts on his neck and ears as he and his men dragged cannons for miles into the wilderness, in search of a fight that never came. His ass of a commander suspected the Huron guide of warning the Mohawk about their movements, too ignorant to know no Huron warrior would aid his most bitter enemy. And the fleet-of-foot Mohawk would always move faster than regiments hauling cannons through swamps.

Lucas had had enough of it. The Mohawk weren't looking for a fight. They wanted to be left alone south of the boundaries others had mapped, wherever the hell those borders were. Every copse of trees looked just like the next. When the commander ordered him to send men to search for the enemy, Lucas handpicked his friends and directed them north, away from conflict. Henri had dropped a wink and led the crew of his brothers-in-war, who'd swaggered off like they were on the way to a tavern. Lucas was sure they'd be safe.

Senseless, all of it.

New world or old, there had to be a better way to resolve conflicts among men.

Marie listened, as patient and calm as a windless day. He let the rest tumble out of him. When the campaign ended and he'd return to Montreal, he'd gone half-mad when he found out his men had never made it back. He'd defied orders to return to his post and set out to find them. He'd stumbled upon them here, weeks later, dead by violence or exposure or sickness or wolves, he didn't know. No clues remained as to the source.

The wilderness had swallowed them up.

"I'm so sorry, Lucas." Marie laid her cheek on his sleeve. "What a terrible loss."

His ribs squeezed with remorse, guilt, blame.

She whispered, "The nightmares aren't just about Flanders, then. They're about what happened here, too."

"Yes."

He never should have sent them away.

He should have died with him.

"But think, Lucas." She ran a glove hand up his sleeve. "If you were among them, buried here, and one of your men—Henri, say, or Jacques—had survived...would you want him to stand over these graves and be tormented? To suffer as you do?"

He flinched at the thought. She spoke a truth he didn't want to hear. He and his men had been soldiers to the core. They honored their fallen comrades together. They'd always known death waited in the shadows. But none of them could imagine what it was like to be the last man standing.

He slid an arm around her. Her hair smelled of rosewater. Her body molded warm against his. He kept forgetting she was a soldier's daughter. He didn't deserve this woman and her understanding of things that should be beyond her knowing. Every day, another truth became clearer: He wanted her to stay with him. Long after spring came. Long after the river ran free. He wanted her by his side through summer and fall and into another winter. He wanted her to keep reading from the books in the bedroom and reminding him his grief didn't belong to him alone. She was a balm that soothed his churning mind.

She made him feel half-human again.

"There's something else you need to know, Marie." Every instinct roared for him to shut his mouth, but a man shouldn't keep secrets from the woman he loves. "Something I didn't tell you before we married."

"Oh?"

"There's more than one reason why I chose to live on this land."

"I can guess at least one reason I didn't know before." She ran a hand across the snow. "For you, this is hallowed ground."

"It's cursed, too." He squinted south, avoiding her eyes, seeing nothing. "It stands between the Huron territory to the north and that of the Mohawks and their brother tribes to the south. The French are aligned with the Huron, the Mohawks are allies of the English. It boils down to this: we're on a border." He reached into the hole and tapped the top of Jacques's cross. "Wherever there's a border...there will be blood."

A breeze sifted through the pines, raining a glittery veil of snow all around them. Marie's brows drew together. He'd probably terrified her, but she deserved to know the truth, his little porcupine.

"Before we married," she said, "you warned me that life in the wilderness would be hard. Moose and bears and deep winter and all that."

"Not war. I didn't talk of war."

"But I read about those dangers, too." She brushed a little more snow away from the hole that marked Henri's grave. "How long ago did you bury these soldiers, Lucas?"

It felt like yesterday, the ache bit so deep. "Six years, three months." He calculated. "Fourteen days."

"So the war is long over."

But the danger would *never* pass. He'd been a soldier since the age of seventeen. He'd never known the world without conflict. He was always guarding, always looking for rising trouble, always expecting the worst.

The world wouldn't change.

Neither would he.

"Let's talk about this later, shall we?" She pushed herself up on her snowshoes and held out her hand. "It's time to go home."

CHAPTER TWENTY-TWO

To Marie, the trip back to the cabin took decades. She was in knots about Lucas's state of mind. He walked as he usually did, raising his chin to eye the landscape left and right, but when his alertness waned, his head hung so low his short beard brushed against his chest.

Were all soldiers who returned from war so damaged?

Her legs wobbled with exhaustion by the time the cabin came into view. Inside, they threw off their ice-encrusted coats, grateful for the reedy warmth of the banked coals. While he rebuilt the fire into a blaze, she fetched bowls and pewter spoons and set herself to the task of nursing his wounded spirit. Filling a bowl from the pot of stew she'd set simmering earlier, she urged Lucas into one of the hearth armchairs and offered it up. He took it, his gaze fathoms deep.

She retreated to the opposite chair, curling her legs up under her, giving Lucas some time to think. She suspected he was still reliving the horrors as if they were still present. A memory drifted back to her, of her father waking every morning to survey the grounds of the manor house, flintlock in hand. Hunting for rabbits, he'd told her, though he always returned empty-handed. Now she found herself wondering if her father had really been seeking snipers in the hedgerows, ten years and a thousand miles from the battle that had scarred him so badly.

She glanced over the bowl of stew at her brooding, silent husband. He was not so far lost as her father had been. Still, she would give him time for his mind to catch up with his body, time to return to this place, to her. She dipped into the bowl of venison stew, surprised to find it rich with gravy and chunks of turnip, delicious and filling, one of her rare successes. She savored it until she'd eaten her fill, putting it aside only when she noticed him stirring into new awareness.

Standing up, she crossed the space between them and slid onto his lap.

"Come back to me, Lucas."

Cupping his bearded jaw, she turned his face to hers. He gazed at her through faraway eyes.

She pressed close, whispering, *It's in the past now.* She brushed her mouth against his until a tremor passed through his body. She pulled away to run a thumb over the ridge of his furrowed brow.

Come back, Lucas.

Come back to me.

Seeing him so lost in grief churned her up inside. She buried her face in his hair.

He ran a hand up her back, murmuring, "After all I told you today, you should be terrified."

She pressed her mouth to the top of his head. "If you'd told me that story before we married, I would have been."

"You wouldn't have agreed to marry me either."

"Isn't that why you kept it to yourself?"

"Yes." He winced. "My lie brought you here."

"And freed me from a jail cell." She smoothed his thick hair off his brow. "I'm glad you lied. I'm a braver woman because of it. I'll always be grateful for that."

He turned his face into her throat. She shifted in his arms like a ship at sea as his chest swelled and deflated. After a while, she felt a tug on the back of her head. The rawhide tie that cinched her braid tumbled across her lap. He loosened her hair and ran his fingers down in long, languorous sweeps.

"Do you remember," he said, in a very different voice than before, "the Huron guide I mentioned, the one my commander didn't trust?"

"Yes." She curled more closely around his body as he stroked her, feeling like a cat nestled in wool.

"His name is Mitameg." He drew his fingertips through tangles, gently. "He visited the trading post, often, exchanging furs for black powder and shot. He always had a story to tell. He once said that if a Huron warrior was wounded, star-maidens would descend from the sky to heal him."

She imagined that, bright stars falling from the milky smear in the velvet sky.

"You're my star maiden, Marie." His voice thickened. "It's like you've been sent from afar."

"What a poet you've become."

A soft prickling began at the back of her eyes. His face bore little resemblance to that of the soldier who'd stepped into Madame Bourdon's parlor months ago, stiff of jaw, hard of eye, blasting an air of authority. She traced a hand down his stubbly cheek, caught up in a rush of feeling. He'd shown her so many kindnesses, now finally she could return some kindness of her own.

She smiled at him in welcome. He would kiss her now. Hunger would rise between them. He would lift her up from the chair and lower them both to the warm hearthstone. They would strip naked as firelight danced over their flesh. By offering herself up, she could bring Lucas the forgetfulness he needed to put those nightmares in the past, where they belonged.

She waited, suspended in stillness. Why wasn't he kissing her yet? She'd never seen such a look in his smoky eyes, or such gentleness on his face. She shifted on his lap, unsettled by the delay. It usually took no more than a wink to encourage him to lay his hands on her. If he didn't touch her soon, her heart would burst out of her chest, as much from confusion as desire.

"Lucas." Even to her ears, her breathless laugh sounded strained. "Are you ever going to kiss me?"

"Patience, *Anentaks.*" His gaze roamed her features. "Let me look my fill."

Her pulse skipped. She glanced away from him but couldn't resist turning back. She didn't know how to behave under such scrutiny. It wasn't as if he never spent time perusing her body. Many a morning, he'd tugged the linens off so he could drink in her nudity. She understood that. It stoked his passion and made her feel so desirable. But he'd never taken the time to observe her quite like this. Desire danced in his eyes, but did so behind a scrim of other feelings. Should she take special care of her expression? Block her scattered thoughts? She set her palm flat against his chest, half-wishing he would stop, half-wishing he would never stop.

A frisson sizzled in the air between them, something new and different and otherworldly. The little hairs on the back of her arms rose. She'd never felt so vulnerable, so exposed, even in the most intimate of intimacies, had never felt so much in tune with his breathing, even when their bodies joined. What was this current passing between them, the pure understanding, the flood of promise?

The answer floated up, unbidden.

Love.

She froze and laid both hands flat on his chest. *Not possible.* Love was more dangerous than beasts of tooth and claw, or bone-chilling winter, or the bloody violence Lucas had confessed to her over his men's graves.

Was she such a fool to make the same mistake twice?

"Marie?"

She gripped his face and kissed him hard. When he tried to disentangle himself, she kissed silent the words he kept trying to say. *Don't ask. Don't say anything.* She pulled on his clothing and tugged on her own, pressing her body against his until he groaned, and surrendered to the passion that overcame them both.

CHAPTER TWENTY-THREE

Lucas knew he couldn't understand a woman's mind. Women were riddles, opaque about what they wanted. Like many a soldier, when he had a burning need for a woman's touch, he preferred to stick to professionals.

Just a lot simpler that way.

But he'd lived with Marie long enough to figure out a few things. After the rough, raucous tumble last night, the one that had nearly overturned the dining table and left a trail of clothes leading into the bed where they now lay, his gut told him she was trying to distract him. That hungry grappling had been her way of cutting off what he'd been about to say. And now in the growing dawn, by faking sleep, he knew for sure she really didn't want to hear it.

She didn't love him.

Why would she?

He was a man in the grip of a violent past, better off left alone.

Staring at the rafters, his heart aching, he forced himself to absorb those truths and think beyond them. He and Marie still had weeks left together. Every primitive instinct urged him to pull her closer and whisper his feelings in her ear, but if he blurted the truth, she would shrink into herself again. She might even insist on putting an end to their agreement right now and demand they sleep in separate rooms. He'd be a fool to destroy what they had.

He would keep his damn mouth shut. And to ease the awkwardness between them, he would use Marie's favorite tactic: playing in bed. After all that had happened back in Paris, Marie could have become a cautious, distrustful, even a bitter woman, for damn good reason. She'd been betrayed to the core, yet she'd made a choice not just to accept, but embrace, her playful, womanly self. So he would coax her back to joy in the only way he knew how.

Then, maybe, she'd stop using their bodies' intimacy as a shield.

He turned on his side and slid the covers down her body to lay a kiss on the sweet indentation of her waist. His hand explored the curve of her hip. Glimpsing a faint blue bruise, no doubt from the wild coupling of the night before, he brushed his lips over it as he ran his fingers toward her sex.

Her lashes fluttered as a moan rose up from her throat. He watched her features as he gently encouraged her excitement. Her thighs went loose at his touch, giving him room to explore. She sucked in a breath as he slid his palm across her pleasure. Her black hair tangled against the pillow.

He wanted every part of her body against his tongue—lips, breasts, the back of her knees—but today, he would give her tender sex the attention it deserved. Sliding under the covers, he eased under her knee and used his shoulders to spread her thighs wide. The musky scent of her desire inflamed his own. He ran a thumb along her cleft before sucking her swollen nub. She responded with the whole of her body, arching her back, pressing her cheek against the pillow, seizing handfuls of furs so her knuckles turned white. Sliding his tongue along her private flesh, he reached up to fill his palms with her breasts.

He could kiss her this way for hours just for the gift of those moans. By the quivering against his mouth, he had only moments before she stiffened with a shout and powerful contractions shuddered her body. When her pleasure did finally crest, waves of it echoed through him, along a rush of triumph. He'd given her this joy. If only he could win her heart with the same skill as he worked her body.

Too much to hope for.

"Lucas!" she gasped, when she went slack, heaving. "Good morning to you, too."

He glanced up, framed between her lovely thighs. She looked down at him from under her wrist, slung across her forehead. His reason tripped. Every time he met those midnight-blue eyes, the dark winter in his heart thawed a little more.

Go easy. Don't scare her.

Everything is just as it was before.

"You were so warm curled up next to me," he said, rising up on his elbows to nip a freckle on her upper thigh. "I couldn't resist."

"Feel free to not resist," she murmured, "any time you please."

"You taste good."

She choked out a laugh. "You must be hungry."

For you. Always.

"Is there something I can do for you?" She pulled a lock of hair away from the corner of her mouth. "You must be ready to burst, you poor thing."

His cock twitched, but he willed it down. "Not now."

"Lucas, you know how I love to return favors."

"I do." By the saints, this woman. He planted another kiss on her thigh and then slid out from under her knee. "But this one was just for you."

She looked confused, and a moment later, wary.

"I don't want to hurt you." He sat up and traced the faint bruise on her hip. "I was too rough on you last night."

"Oh, that?" Her voice dropped, but only a fraction of the wariness eased. "You didn't hear me complaining."

"All the same." He dragged the linens over her flushed thighs and up to her breasts. "I'll try not to be a wild bear when I mate with you from now on."

"How disappointing." She narrowed her eyes. "Still, I like the way you apologize."

Mischief danced across her face, washing away the last of her wariness. She'd forgiven him, then, for his roughness last night.

Or maybe she was just as willing as he to push from her memory how close he came to speaking words of love.

"I'm starving." Tapping her pretty, rounded bottom, he swung his legs over the side of the bed. "Any of that stew left?"

Keep her happy, Lucas thought.

What else could he do?

That night, he made her ice skates from the shin bones of deer. Later in the week, he taught her how to use them in a shallow bay of the frozen river. As the temperature ticked up to a more comfortable chill, they explored eastward and found a long, low slope that formed a natural, treeless valley. The next day, they brought an oiled deerskin and enjoyed an afternoon of sledding. He imagined, now and again, he glimpsed a softer look in her eyes as the days rolled into weeks. But maybe that was just her dreaming—not of him, but of returning to her friends and her safer life in the Paris convent. The words *I love you* hovered on his lips every morning, *stay with me* surged in his throat every evening.

He swallowed the words down. He'd be an empty husk of a man if she said no.

Then, one day, the ice broke on the St. Lawrence River.

"Good morning, Lucas."

Lucas turned away from the spectacle of the churning river to the vision of Marie on the porch, dressed in moose skin breeches and fur boots.

His ribs squeezed.

"I'm ready." She thrust her hand into a glove, though the weather was balmy compared to the weeks prior. "What are we doing today?"

"Tapping maple trees." He gestured toward the woods. "We'll start with the ones behind the cabin."

"Ah, yes, those magical trees that ooze sugar."

"It's sap, not sugar, *Anentaks*." He set his foot on the path. "And the trees are only magical in Huron tales."

"Nonsense." She squinted up at the drifting clouds. "Remember those green lights we saw weaving in the night sky last month? Or the two red foxes yesterday, frolicking like something out of *Aesop's Fables*? This place is full of magic, and you know it."

She smiled at him, leaning in. A blessed saint couldn't resist what she offered. He dipped his head and kissed her as if she would always be his, as if the river that led back to Quebec didn't rush and gurgle louder than ever before. When he pulled away, the smolder of her evening-blue gaze turned his insides out.

Ah, Marie.

I want so much more than your body.

"We've got work to do." He gently pinched her chin. "Come, I'll show you the magic trees."

She all but skipped, peppering him with questions about the names of other trees, of the birds singing in the boughs, and whether he'd seen the doe and two fawns she'd glimpsed yesterday drinking by the river's edge. He answered her questions when he could, but talk of the river put a boulder in his gullet.

"Here we are." He halted by a maple where he'd left a pile of buckets. "We'll start with this one."

"It doesn't look magical." She frowned up at the plain, leafless tree. "How do you know it's a maple?"

"I marked it in autumn, when it still had leaves." He tugged on a tattered ribbon around the lower trunk, caked with wet mud. "The leaves of sugar maples turn many colors."

"Ah, yes. I think I saw them among the pines when I first sailed into Quebec."

"Even if I hadn't marked the tree," he continued, dodging talk about Quebec, or ships, or sailing away, "I could still recognize a maple." He pulled down a branch to show her one of the dried buds and droned on about maples until his throat tired of talking.

"Here." He pulled a carved chute out of his satchel. "Hold this."

As she held it, he took a mallet and nail from his sack of tools. Setting the sharp end at an angle against the trunk, he tapped a hole into the tree. Retrieving the chute from her hand, he shoved it into the angled hole. A drip soon formed and ran down the chute's center furrow.

"That's the syrup?" she said, a little ridge rising between her brows. "It looks like water."

"It'll thicken when it's boiled." He scooped a translucent drop and held out his finger. "Taste it."

Her hot mouth slid down over his knuckle. His body pulsed while her lips pulled back, tight on his skin.

My body is yours, yours is mine.

But will you ever give me your heart?

"There are sixty more trees to tap," he warned, retrieving his finger from her mouth. "You'll be picking mud out of your hair for the rest of the morning if you don't stop teasing."

Her eyes gleamed with mischief. "It's not very sweet, that syrup."

"It will be, after it's boiled down."

He pounded another nail into the tree, above the chute, from which to hang a pail. Melting snow kept dripping from the bare branches, leaving little holes in the ice-crust all around them. Deeper in the woods, clods of wet snow slid from the upper boughs of pines and splattered to the ground.

How much longer could he pretend spring wasn't coming?

"Teach me, Lucas."

He breathed in the scent of her, warm woman, wet moose leather. "Teach you what? How to tap a tree?"

"How to make the syrup."

"It's a boring job." *Though I'd like to see you stirring the pot, Anentaks, with the spring sun shining on your hair.* "You have to keep an eye on the mess so as not to over-boil."

"Boring is fine. I'd like to see this maple-sugar thing through to the end."

He shoved his hand in the satchel and gripped a chute tight. A splinter pierced his hand. She didn't know what she was asking. Making syrup meant waiting until they'd collected enough sap to fill a pot. That could take weeks, perhaps a whole month beyond the coming of spring, depending on the trees and the caprices of weather.

His heart ached with indecision. Should he steal that time, another bite of heaven, before he had to fulfill his promise? And if she hadn't fallen in love with him by now, what made him think he'd succeed, even if he kept her until the trees ran bone dry?

"Hold this." He yanked out of his satchel another chute. "We'll talk about boiling the syrup later."

CHAPTER TWENTY-FOUR

Marie didn't care a whit about boiling syrup. She was just nudging him, seeing if Lucas would broach the subject she couldn't bring herself to mention. That little matter of the ice-free river, and the promise he'd made to her five months ago.

She couldn't live another day with this uncertainty.

Not another hour.

Returning to the cabin on the excuse of making dinner, Marie set to work, but the pressure kept building and building behind her chest. These last few weeks, she'd struggled to push aside fear and face her tangled emotions, but the battle never ended.

She was a fool to think she was in love, Paris had taught her that, but what else could these feelings be? Fortunately, Lucas hadn't looked at her in that unsettling way again. He'd woken the next day acting like nothing untoward had happened.

She'd followed his lead, grateful for it...but, in truth, she was crawling out of her skin. How she wished Cecile was here. Cecile would understand her terror; Ceci would know what she should do. As it was, Marie could only summon up Ceci's advice from long ago, words that kept ringing in her head.

Are you sure, in the deepest, deepest part of your heart, that this man is honest and good?

Yes.

Yes.

The certainty curled her toes, for it was based on five months of living with the man. Her feelings for Francois shrank to childish imaginings in comparison. But still... She wondered if Genny felt as certain about the devotion of her woods-roaming husband. Why else would her friend risk the terrors of the wilderness, if not for love?

Oh, to be that brave.

Setting the table, she lit the last of the beeswax candles Philippe had packed in the canoe five months ago. She lifted the lid of the stew, stirring it before knocking the gravy off the wooden spoon and returning the lid. She'd stoked the hearth fire to take the chill out of the air and brushed her hair until it gleamed. Changing out of her wilderness clothing, she ran her hands down the skirts of the blue brocade dress, her wedding dress, hoping she looked beguiling and irresistible rather than a wreck of nervous energy.

The heavy creak of Lucas's footsteps kicked up her pulse. He fussed on the porch for a while, washing his hands, knocking the mud off his boots, while she tried to control her jitteriness. When he opened the door, she nearly lost her resolve. To think she'd once given herself away because of a rolling laugh and pair of handsome black eyes. Ignorant of deeper feelings, she'd mistaken Francois's good looks and joviality for something far more profound.

Love sizzled to ash if not fed with patience and kindness and trust.

"The stew smells good." Lucas's voice dropped deep. "You smell better."

A trill coiled through her. How easy it would be to fall into his arms. A bout of lovemaking would put both of them in an agreeable mood, but she knew that was just a way to defer the inevitable.

She couldn't be a coward any longer.

"Lucas." Her stomach hollowed. "We have to talk."

He stilled in the way he did in the woods when he heard a crack of a twig.

She said, "It's about our agreement."

Expressions shifted over his face like swift-moving clouds, too quick to read. He dipped his head and unbuttoned his coat. "So you've seen it."

"Seen...what?"

"The river."

Ah, that. "Yes. I have."

She pressed a hand against her stomach. She had stood by the churning waterway this very afternoon, her feelings running faster than the current, roiling more than the foaming whitewater. Were Lucas's feelings for her as deep as this river, or was she imagining devotion when all he offered was kindness?

"The river is dangerous." Lucas set his coat on a peg with an excess of care. "The spring melt hasn't passed its peak, and the water is still freezing. I won't risk an overturned canoe."

The excuses seemed logical, they tilted her off her intent. She was so swamped with emotions, she'd forgotten he might respond with rational thought.

She asked, "How long, then?"

He glared at her, the old, baffled, knife-silver glare he used to shoot at her in the early days.

She prodded, "One day more? A week?"

"I'll take you when it's safe." His brows drew together. "I won't break my promise."

A chasm yawned inside her. *What if I want you to break it?*

"Did you think I'd forgotten, Marie?" His voice, gruff. "A man stands by his word, or his word is wind."

"So you'll bring me back to Quebec. No hesitation."

"If you want to go home—" he yanked off his hat, tousling his hair "—I'll see it done."

She stepped toward the table and seized the back of a chair to keep upright. "Yes, I want to be home." She swallowed a sob. "More than anything."

Those words weren't quite what she meant, she regretted them the moment they left her mouth. The idea of home had changed. Once, home was the manor house she shared with her father, the one with the rope swing in the back yard. Then home became the orphanage, the camaraderie of her friends, and the kindness of the nuns. Now home was *here,* in this cabin that always smelled like pine, in Lucas's world of trees, in Lucas's strong arms.

He stood just inside the door, his stance stubbornly fixed. He might as well be across a sea. His throat worked, like he was trying to summon words. She waited, mentally begging him to speak so she wouldn't have to. She squeezed her eyes shut, warding off her own faint-heartedness. She'd vowed to be the one confessing. A hundred thousand words pressed behind her throat, but she supposed they all boiled down to one single truth, riding just ahead of tears.

"I've been thinking on this, Lucas."

Stone-cold quiet, her husband.

"For days, weeks, I've tried to imagine being back behind the stone walls of my old orphanage."

How could he just stand there, as straight as a soaring pine?

"E-every time I do," she stuttered, "those walls turn into pine woods in my mind."

"That'll change." His jaw shifted. "Once you get back to Paris, you'll forget this place ever existed."

"How could I ever forget?" She clutched her arms in a vain effort to shield her sore heart. "I love the clear, clean smell of snow. I love the blue of the sky, and the way the river gurgles under the ice. These past months I've felt so...alive. Paris is no longer my home." She braced herself. "My home is with you."

He shuddered like a pine struck with an ax.

"Are you saying—" he stopped on a sucked-in breath "—you don't want to leave?"

"Yes."

The word rang in the air, pure truth.

"You would live here?" His gaze sharpened. "In this lonely place? With me?"

"Not so lonely when I'm in your arms."

She heard a soft, whooshing sound—his hat, tumbling to the floor. He closed the space between them in two steps and cupped her cheeks.

"Say it." His fingers pressed into her. "I need to hear it, Marie."

She'd said so many things. She couldn't remember half of them, not while Lucas looked at her with such intensity. His astonished expression gave her courage to speak the words she'd feared most, and had saved for last.

"I love you, Lucas."

Oof.

Her feet left the ground as he hauled her up against him.

"I'd lost hope." He pressed his forehead against hers. "I thought you didn't want this. I thought you didn't want me."

"There's nothing I want more."

"I would have done anything you asked. Even put you on a ship, if that's what it took to make you happy."

"I'm happy with *you.*"

"You're my heart, Anentaks. I've known this for so long but didn't want to scare you away."

Her mind went bright. She touched his face to make sure she wasn't a foolish girl dreaming.

"Say it," she whispered.

"I love you." He squeezed her close. "Now marry me."

She laughed. "We *are* married."

"Then promise you'll be my forever wife."

"I do."

His kiss tasted of maple. Those kisses multiplied and deepened until her senses fled.

He stopped only to rest his forehead against hers. Laughter bubbled up between them. His was low and rumbling, she'd never heard it so free.

She kissed him again, with deeper intent. Above the sound of her own breathlessness, she thought she heard a faint explosion, like a cork popping off a bottle of fermenting apple cider. A shattering of glass and a thud followed, but she was so lost in Lucas, she wondered if she imagined it all. In her mind, fireworks were bursting into colors, like the ones she'd once seen against the night sky as a girl, when Louis XIV had returned to Paris from his castle in Versailles.

Then the pop, crash, and thud happened again. This time accompanied by a blazing heat as a lead ball whistled through her hair.

CHAPTER TWENTY-FIVE

The crack of a rifle kicked Lucas to high alert. He shoved Marie to the floor and blocked her.

"Lucas!"

He pressed a finger against her mouth. Over his shoulder, he eyed the shattered corner of the window and then searched the walls until he saw a charred chip in the stone, still smoking with spent saltpeter. The shooter had aimed from the northeast side of the cabin. A padded muffle of running footsteps outside confirmed his suspicions. More than one shooter, he thought, listening. More than two.

Three men were in a killing mood.

Keep Marie alive.

He nudged her under the table, positioning his body between the woman he loved and any new shot of lead. Reaching up, he patted the tablecloth in search of a knife, found it, and brought it down to show it to her.

"Take it," he whispered. "Crawl to that wall and keep crawling beneath the windows until you reach the bedroom. Bolt the door and hide between the bed and the wall—"

"Lucas, no—"

"I don't know who's out there." Light gleamed on the steel blade. "But if one of them gets past me, don't hesitate to use this."

She shrank back, went pale.

"Aim for the eyes, throat, groin." He pressed his lips into her hair. "You're strong, Anentaks. Stay calm."

She took the knife from his hand. He released her and rolled free so she could scramble to her knees. Tucking her skirts into her belt, she kept low and crawled toward the bedroom. Her hand slipped on the handle twice before she managed to open the door and crawl in. His heart went with her.

Only then did he surrender to his soldier's instincts. The first shot had not been a warning. Whoever was out there wanted them both dead.

On his belly, he scooted over to seize his rifle, powder horn, and bag of shot. He slid again through shattered glass to position himself beside the ripped oilskin of the broken window. Checking the barrel of the gun, he loaded it, pulled the ramrod, and drove the powder and ball in tight. Outside, a porch floorboard creaked. He knew exactly which floorboard. He aimed the loaded gun in the space between window and shade, nudging the oilskin with the bore to see what was coming. In the twilight, he glimpsed a crouched silhouette. He raised his head to get a keener look at the enemy and paused.

"Put down the weapon and identify yourself." He peered down the length of the iron bore to aim. "Don't make me shoot you."

The crouching enemy swung up his flintlock. Lucas cursed and squeezed the trigger of his own. More window glass shattered. Shrapnel scored his forehead. Outside, porch boards groaned as a weight tumbled off.

He reloaded as warm blood ran down his cheek.

He yelled, "Who's next?"

A flaming torch sailed through the window. A rifle barrel soon followed. Lucas shoved the barrel away as it discharged. Seizing the hot bore, Lucas drove the gun hard through the window to knock down the owner. Leaping to his feet, he swept up the torch and flung it toward the hearth before he charged out the front door.

The man he'd knocked still struggled to his feet. Lucas hurled himself across the porch to slam his body into him. The enemy cursed in perfect French as they tumbled into the mud. Twilight flashed on steel. Lucas grabbed the wrist that held the glinting knife and saw, on his attacker's face, an eye of milky blue.

Realization struck him.

Fortin.

The murdering Frenchman had come for vengeance—with his cousin, Lucas realized, as the sound of a scraping ramrod came from behind. Lucas rolled over to see Landry tipping powder into the pan of a rifle now aimed at his face.

Time slowed as he stared down the black bore of a newly-loaded weapon. Eternity stretched between the seconds. He'd been in this still, ringing place before. Dozens of times, two continents apart. Life hung by a thread when a gun was pointed so close. He could fight, if he still had it in him. But death was the effortless choice, as easy as surrender, and just as seductive. The thought teased him, winked familiarly, an old friend beckoning. Then he realized: he'd been waiting for death to come. He'd been preparing for a very long time.

No.

That was before Marie.

His wife, helpless in the cabin.

Now, he never wanted to live so badly.

With a slap of a hand, he deflected the bore as Landry's gun fired. Jerking up, he stomped Fortin in the ribs and turned on the other Frenchman with bloody intent. A fighting madness took over.

He became all motion, no thought but survival.

Much later, the blood-haze of the fight thinned behind his eyes. A chill painted the back of his throat. He heaved heavy, hard breaths. One leg tingled with pin-sharp cold. The other flowed with warm blood. He could see only narrowly out of one eye, but well enough to make out the shapes sprawled motionless on the ground around him. He nudged them. None moved.

He raised his gaze, surveying the twilight darkening to the gloaming for more enemies. Flashes of the fight played across his mind. The crack of knuckles against bone. Flintlock-blasts. A rolling torch.

Marie.

He twisted toward the cabin. Ice-sharp spears shot through him, radiating down his back, but he ignored it for now. No flames leaped beyond the windows, no sparks rose from the roof. His toss of the torch toward the hearth must have tumbled true. On the porch, he glimpsed a woman's shape. She grasped a weapon, the bore pointed down. Relief, iced with fear, showered over him. *She's safe.* He lurched toward her, staring at her through his one good eye, seeking any sign of injury. She stood in simple grace, as if she'd descended from the clouds.

His star maiden.

His wife.

The bore of her flintlock knocked the porch boards as he approached.

"Lucas." Her eyes went wide. "There's a knife in your shoulder."

Marie held her breath as Lucas mumbled something through a split lip, some ridiculously common thing about going inside the cabin so she wouldn't be cold. As if her shivering was the worst of what had just happened. It astounded her he was standing upright after the blows she'd seen him take, the wrestling she'd witnessed, the knife she'd watched flashing in the dying light. Now he winced as he reached over his shoulder in search of the hilt. When he knocked it with clumsy fingers, his body stiffened.

"Stop," she said. "You're making it worse."

He dropped his hand. "You'll have to pull it out."

Impossible. She couldn't do that. She wasn't a surgeon. And yet, only moments ago, she'd smothered a torch fire with bed linens and her own skirts. Moments ago, she'd loaded a flintlock and aimed to kill.

Her stomach lurched, splashing the back of her throat with bile. She swallowed it down and pointed Lucas inside. "Go sit by the hearth."

"Not there." He swayed like a pine in a blizzard. "In the bedroom."

Lucas limped inside. She followed, leaning the still-smoking rifle against the wall with shaky hands. Lucas shuffled to the hearth to grab a wooden spoon from a canister on the mantel. A mad sort of laugh bubbled up in her—*are you going to help me cook?*—but the laugh died fast as he tested the wooden handle between his teeth.

He headed toward the bedroom, saying, "Bring scissors."

The wave of bile surged a little higher. She headed to her sewing basket on leaden feet and rifled up the scissors. When she joined him in the bedroom, He was already sitting on the bed's edge. She climbed up behind him. The knife, welling with blood, pinned his clothes to his body, so she snipped the leather of his jerkin and linen of his shirt away. She trimmed carefully, as if she could sew up the deerskin later, as if a few stitches would make everything right again.

Panic threatened, but she choked it down as she pulled the cloth free of the weapon.

"It was Fortin," he said, his voice thick. "And Landry."

She already knew. When she'd peeked through the bedroom window at the sound of men grappling, she'd seen a flash of Fortin's demonic face. "There was a third man, too."

"Yes, the first shooter." His lids drifted closed and jerked open again. "A hired killer, I can only guess. The cousins wanted to make sure the odds were in their favor."

"Save your strength, Lucas." The men were dead, better to focus on what they had to do now. "Can you lie on your stomach?"

He shifted his legs onto the bed and eased down, turning his head on the pillow as he lay flat. The knife hilt jutted out of his shoulder at an angle.

Impossible, this.

"Two hands," he muttered, his eyelids sinking. "Pull it out at...the angle it went in. Straight and steady."

"And after?" *There will be an after.*

"Cover the wound. Press hard." He shifted his body and grunted, his muscles bunching against a jolt of pain. "Just...stop the bleeding."

Her hands went numb. She flexed them to force feeling back.

"I've been hurt worse, Anentaks." He fumbled for the wooden spoon he'd set on the commode table. "You can do this."

He set the handle between his teeth. She positioned her hands on the hilt of the knife. The chill of the ivory against her palm startled her, kicking up a memory. She'd gripped another knife once before, in a similar moment of terror, with her future hanging in the balance.

Lucas was her future now.

He *had* to live.

She hauled on the bloody knife until it budged. Lucas made an inhuman sound around the wooden handle clenched between his teeth. She gripped harder and gave another pull as his body seized and then went limp. The spoon handle fell out of his mouth just as she fell back on the bed, the blade free.

Clattering the weapon onto the commode table, she tugged on the bed linens and pressed a wad atop the bleeding wound. His upper torso rose and fell under her hands, proof he was still breathing. She put her weight into the pressure, praying with new fervency. *Don't die, Lucas. Please don't die.* Her wrists grew sore, her shoulders ached, and a splotch of blood soaked the linens.

When she couldn't press any longer, she gently lifted the linen. It hadn't completely stopped bleeding, but the flow had slowed. She laid fresh linens on the wound and tied fabric around his shoulders to keep the cloth in place.

Sliding off the bed, she kneeled beside it. "Lucas?" His eyes didn't open. "Lucas…tell me what to do."

A lock of hair had fallen over his forehead. She ran her fingers through it, combing it off his face. His breathing was labored, but steady. It would be a while, she realized, before Lucas would be able to tell her anything.

Stay calm, he'd told her before.

Don't be afraid.

She gathered her wits and assessed the blood splatter all over his clothes. She didn't know whether it was his or that of his enemies, but she knew she had to find out. She pulled and tugged at his clothing until she found a dozen slashes, still beading blood. Fortin had been a deadly artist with his knife's edge. She cleaned the smaller wounds, bound the deeper ones, and then covered him to keep him warm. When she finished, she pressed her nose against his hair, closing her eyes against tears.

She would be his star maiden now.

She wouldn't fail him.

Squaring her shoulders, she stepped into the chaos of the parlor. She put away the dinner dishes and swept up the broken glass. A howl from the far distance wasn't a new sound in the winter night, but Lucas had taught her predators were drawn to the scent of blood. A chill slid down her spine. Bracing herself, she stepped outdoors and eyed the three dead men sprawled under the light of the newly-risen moon. Slinging the rifle across her back, she retrieved Lucas's deer sled from the barn and got to work. One at a time, she rolled the bodies onto the sled and dragged them into the barn. Moonlight helped her keep an eye out for wolves. It also illuminated the bullet wound in Landry's side.

Her aim had been true.

She'd killed a man. Her stomach roiled. She managed to keep herself from emptying the contents until after her grim task was done.

She couldn't think about that. There was too much to do. She passed the night checking on Lucas and stretching a new deerskin over the window. She plugged the ragged hole in the glass with rags. As morning dawned, she changed his dressings and made him drink water when he rose into a hazy awareness. He was doing better, she told herself. His muttering was just the nightmares returning, prompted by the bloody fight. With him abed, she had to take care of more than just food, so she ventured outside to collect maple sap. Stepping across wolf prints that had imprinted circles around the bloody splotches on the snow, she brought in extra wood for the fire, made a fresh batch of sagamité, and coaxed Lucas every few hours into drinking a few sips of water.

That night, sleet pattered on the roof, lulling her into an exhausted sleep.

She woke up to Lucas in a sweaty delirium. Panic knocked at the shield of her courage. In the orphanage, fever heralded agues and plagues and the wooden-wheel creak of the tumbrels. She backed out of the bedroom, flung the front door open, and bolted toward the river to think. At the muddy bank she paced, peering up and down, praying for a canoe to appear. Fur-traders heading to the settlements to trade, Celeste and her stepson returning for a visit, that band of Abenaki Lucas had once promised would pass through. When no canoe came, she glared up beyond the treetops. But the clouds kept scudding by, offering up no wisdom for how to save the man who had taught her not all men were monsters, and love, *true love*, was not an impossible dream.

The birds kept twittering. The mighty river gurgled by. She watched a tree branch floated past with a sparrow perched atop it, fluffing its feathers. The wood rose and dipped on the current. A current that buoyed every spinning leaf right past her…toward the settlement of Quebec.

CHAPTER TWENTY-SIX

In his dream, Lucas woke to the sight of a nun in a white wimple.

"There you are." The nun reared back and called over her shoulder, "Madame, come quickly. His eyes have opened."

The nun receded in a rustle. He closed his eyes against a wave of weariness. When he opened them again, a lovelier face came into focus.

Marie.

"Lucas, Lucas." Her kiss warmed his sore lip. "I've been waiting for days for you to come back to me."

Anentaks. His arms were pinned under something, too heavy to lift, his throat as parched as old leather.

"Here." She reached for something. "Drink."

A cup appeared before him. In his dream, he pushed upright, collapsing when a sharp pain plunged from his neck to the middle of his back. Angelic Marie leaned over to fuss around him—her scolding words tinny in his ears. He became vaguely aware of soft pillows, stiff linens, and the crunch of a hay-filled mattress. He laid in a bed...his bed? It didn't seem so. Not big enough. Something wasn't...right. His head spun.

It hurt just to think.

She placed the rim of the cup against his mouth. He sipped, and cool water coated the rawness of his throat. It felt so real he sipped more eagerly, until there was no more and she took it away.

He tested his throat. "Where...are we?"

"In the Hotel-Dieu." She refilled the cup from a pewter jug. "The nuns have been taking very good care of you."

"A hospital?"

"Yes."

Lucas blinked and looked beyond dream-Marie. Light flooded in through narrow windows. He saw a row of beds, wooden crosses on the walls, and sisters in gray habits bustling about. *Augustinian nuns.* Like the ones who ran the hospital in Quebec. The thought jolted him. Quebec was far away. The ice had barely cleared the river. The last he remembered, he'd just come home to a cabin filled with candlelight—

The cabin.

Gunfire.

Blood.

"Easy, Lucas." Marie laid a hand on his arm. "We're safe now."

"You're alive." His palms ached to touch her, prove she was real, but his body screamed with every movement. "You're breathing."

She laughed as she set the cup aside. "It was you who was stabbed, my love. Not me."

He drank in the sight of her, the shine on her hair, the freckle high on her cheekbone, the lashes clumped with tears. She radiated brightness and energy and pulsing, vibrant life. She was alive, but behind his closed eyes, he re-fought the skirmish, flinching with each blow.

"Lucas, be calm." A furrow deepened between her brows. "You're breathing so hard."

He battled to clear his mind. He'd put her in danger bringing her to the cabin. He'd been a fool to hope danger might have passed. A jagged edge of guilt unfurled inside him.

She spoke in a low, easy voice. "The doctor says you're as strong as an ox. He'd never seen a man recover so quickly from such wounds." She sat back, fussing with the skirts of a dress he'd never seen before. What happened to the blue one? "He said it shouldn't be more than a few days, and you'll be up and walking. Then we can go back to our cabin."

Our cabin.

He closed his eyes. He had once hoped she would still be in his cabin when the spring rain pattered on the roof. He'd once dared to dream of her bathed in sunlight as she walked across the green summer grass. He'd once yearned to see her swollen with his child in the autumn, as the wind tossed golden leaves across the porch.

What a fool he'd been.

"I'm sorry, Marie."

"Why?" She reached for his hand and slipped her slim fingers between his. "There's nothing to be sorry for."

"There will be, after I say my piece."

"Lucas, we have so much to talk about, but not now, while you're still in pain. When you're back on your feet, we'll have all the time in the world to make plans and—"

"We won't."

Confusion rippled across her face.

"You can't stay in the cabin with me." By the saints, it hurt even to breathe. "It's too dangerous."

She sighed, smiling. "We've talked about this. The nightmares are back, aren't they?"

"I didn't dream up Landry and Fortin."

"Did the nuns give you that awful tisane?" She fingered the bottles on the table beside the bed. "One of these medicines made you so restless—"

"Listen to me." A fresh wave of weakness threatened to sink him. "Someday, another bullet will come through the cabin window. It will be aimed at my heart."

He could tell she was losing patience. Around them, people coughed, sheets rustled, hay mattresses crackled as patients changed positions. Sharp boot heels clicked against the slate floor as nuns made the rounds.

"Once a soldier, always a soldier." She covered his hand, engulfed it in warmth. "I love you for that."

His eyelids weighed like lead. "You're my heart, too, Marie. But I'm still sending you back to Paris."

He saw the kiss coming but was too weary to stop it. She tasted of morning and the metallic tang of cold water from a stream. She tasted like a thousand nights of shared pleasure. He would take this kiss into his dreams and love this woman until the day he died.

The world faded as sleep overcame him.

When he opened his eyes again, the image of Marie was burned behind his eyelids, but his wife was no longer leaning over him. He couldn't tell how much time had passed, only that the shadows in the room had shifted. The rafters were lit up by sun streaming through the narrow windows.

"Lucas?"

He turned his head against the pillow. Pain shot down his back again, but duller than before. Philippe sat on the chair by the bed, the black curls of his wig oiled to a ridiculous sheen.

"You look like hell," Philippe said. "But it's damn good to see you alive."

Lucas pushed himself to a sitting position, wincing, but feeling stronger. "Where is she?"

"At my house, under Etta's care."

His friend leaned forward, offering a cup of what looked like wine. Lucas seized it and drank it to the dregs.

"You won't be seeing Marie any time soon, I'm afraid." Philippe splashed a little more wine into the cup. "Your wife is banned from visiting you here."

"Banned?" He wiped his mouth. "Why?"

"The nuns think she agitates you. You've been waking up shouting her name, throwing fists, and kicking off your bedclothes. The sisters had to restrain you twice."

Lucas's heart squeezed. He'd been dreaming of Marie. New nightmares more terrifying than the old.

"So it's true." Philippe took a sip straight out of the wine bottle. "You fell in love with her."

Lucas turned his face away.

"It's written all over her face, too." Philippe kicked his mud-caked boots on the bed and tilted chair on the back two legs. "What a pair, you two."

"We won't be a pair for long. I want you to buy passage for her on a ship back to France."

"I will not." His dark eyes narrowed. "You'll change your mind."

"I won't. She needs to go back to where she belongs." *Even if the thought of her leaving is a knife in my gut.* "In Paris."

"Keep shouting about sending your wife back to Paris and the news will soon reach Talon's ears." Philippe dropped his feet off the bed as his chair hit the floorboards. "There'll be hell to pay, then—"

"I don't give a damn about Talon."

Philippe sighed hard. "Marie's right. The fever has addled your mind."

He had no fever, not anymore. And Philippe, a soldier himself, should understand more than anyone. "What would Fortin and Landry have done to Marie, if they'd killed me?"

"She would have shot one of them and fought the other tooth and nail."

He shook his head. All the quills in the world wouldn't have saved his *Anentaks*. "She would have lost that fight, and you know it."

"I'm not so sure." Philippe gave him a skeptical eye. "You took a frightened girl into the wilderness and turned her into a frontierswoman—"

"If you won't purchase a berth for her on my account, then I'll do it once I get out of this place."

"Damn it, Lucas." The scar on Philippe's face whitened. "That woman pulled a knife out of your back. She saved your life."

"And I'm trying to save hers."

"Tell me, then." Philippe planted his elbows on his knees and surged forward. "How did you make it here to Quebec? How did you get to this hospital?"

"You found us." The words had no sooner left his mouth before he doubted them. "Of course it was you. You were supposed to keep an eye on Landry and Fortin here in Quebec—"

"I did."

"When they went missing, you followed."

"You're making a lot of assumptions, soldier."

"You're telling me it wasn't you who came to the cabin and brought me here?"

"Yes, that's what I'm telling you. I was sleeping comfortably in my home with my *six* children—and yes, thank you for the congratulations on the recent birth of my son. Why was my mind so at ease, you ask? Because my men reported that Fortin and

Landry were drinking merrily at the tavern, on the very night you were attacked. Imposters, as I recently came to know." Philippe looked ready to take Lucas's throat in his hands. "So *think*. You must remember something about how you got here."

Lucas frowned, confused. Beyond the battle with the cousins, his memory was murky, everything was tangled, disconnected. She'd pulled the knife from his back. That was his last clear memory. Everything else was jumbled like a dream. Except for the rumble of birch bark under his cheek, the buck and roll of a canoe, and, most of all, the lull of a woman's low, steady voice.

No.

It couldn't be.

"Your wife saved your life twice, my friend. She isn't someone who's going to leave without a fight." Philippe tossed the wine bladder so it landed on his chest. "When it comes down to a battle of wills between you two, my money is on Marie."

CHAPTER TWENTY-SEVEN

"Marie!" Marie turned toward the voice to see Etta waving as her friend walked down the hill from the upper town of Quebec. Etta's four-month-old son Mathis curled in a sling around her body. The sight of the babe brought both a wave of warmth and a pinch to her heart.

Etta clucked her tongue. "Oh, my darling girl."

Opening her arms for an embrace, Etta left just enough room for the small, warm body tucked in the sling between them. Separating moments later, Etta used her thumbs to clear the tears from Marie's cheeks with motherly efficiency.

Etta said, "Courage, *ma petite*."

A laugh grazed Marie's throat. "Perhaps I've used it all up."

"That's not true, and you know it."

Marie mustered a smile. Nearly a week had passed since she'd spoken to Lucas, but Philippe kept her appraised of her husband's growing strength...and continued commitment to send her away. Her ribs hurt from trying stifling sobs. What could she do about a man who confessed he loved her and in the very same breath insisted he would send her away? She'd been thinking about that long, and hard, which was how she found herself here in the lower town, pacing between the looming granite promontory and wide stretch of the Saint Lawrence River.

"I need your advice, Etta." Marie squinted toward the riverbank. "Which one should I choose?"

Etta's questioning gaze fell upon the birch-bark vessels pulled up in the mud.

"I thought I'd buy one of them." *Or steal one, if I must.* "Then I could thwart Lucas from shipping me to France by paddling away and hiding from him until the river freezes again."

"Marie, my darling—"

"But Lucas would just hunt me down, wouldn't he? He'd track me to Cecile's home in Trois-Rivières, if Ceci could even take me in—"

"*Petite*," Etta interrupted in the firm but affectionate way she addressed misbehaving children. "You know why Lucas is saying such things."

"He's protecting me."

"It's more than that." Etta took in the bustle of the lower town as if in search of answers. "Have you considered the idea that Lucas is terrified?"

Marie flicked a hand. "Lucas isn't afraid of anything."

"Men swagger to *look* fearless, all the more when they're deeply troubled."

"I've seen him fight—"

"Fighting is easy. He's been trained to fight. But fists and flintlocks can't beat away strong feelings."

"Etta, I know he loves me. He doesn't hesitate to tell me so." She threw up her hands. "Yet he still wants to send me away."

"Because too many of his loved ones have died." Etta tugged on the sling to keep the sun out of the baby's eyes. "It's not my place to talk of such things, Marie. But Lucas lost many soldiers—"

"I know. They're buried on the land."

Etta nodded and lightly bounced the bundle in her arms. "So he told you about the campaign into Mohawk territory."

"You knew, too?"

"Philippe was part of it, too. Lucas stayed with us after he found his men. His wounds didn't need linen and salve, but they were deep."

"You never told me that."

Etta shrugged. "You were with us only a few days before your marriage, Marie. And how am I to tell a bride such a thing? Besides, I'd hoped he'd learned how to live with the loss by now. I had three fewer children when Lucas came, broken in spirit, into my home."

She remembered Lucas at the graveside of his men. If she hadn't known better, she would have thought he still had dirt under his fingernails from digging the graves.

"Soldiers are closer than brothers, you know." Etta's black, winged brows came together. "When one of their friends dies, the soldiers who survive wrestle with terrible guilt."

"I know." Marie remembered her father and the drinking that led to his death. She remembered Lucas shouting and thrashing in his sleep. She remembered Francois, too, that wretched musketeer, and the thought gave her pause. Perhaps, at the root of Francois's greediness for pleasure, women, and drink, lay a great, unspoken agony.

Maybe it was a miracle that all soldiers didn't become monsters.

She whispered, "Do you think Lucas will change his mind, Etta?"

"I don't know, *ma petite*." Etta tilted her face to the reedy warmth of the sun. "He's not wrong about the danger. There will always be threats in this settlement. The Huron and Abenaki have been our allies for decades, but alliances could shift. So could the peace with the English and the Dutch. This colony is no place for the faint-hearted."

"Neither is Paris."

Paris, where her distant family chose to send her to an orphanage rather than raise her as their own. Paris, where men in wigs and pomade decided it was worth the risk of a sea voyage to make her a brood mare for their colonial schemes. Paris, where, in her desperation, she'd thrown herself into the arms of a wolf.

"I'm not faint-hearted." She spoke loudly enough to turn a few heads, but she said the words again anyway. "I am not faint-hearted, Etta."

Etta smiled. "Do *you* believe it, finally?"

"I won't leave here, no matter what Lucas says. Life without love is a kind of death, too."

Etta's eyes gleamed. "Here you are, then. A true Québécois."

A flush rose to her skin, along with new determination. "I have to speak to Lucas."

"Yes." Etta laid a hand on her wrist. "That's why I came to find you. Lucas has just been removed from the hospital."

"Oh?" Her pulse leapt. "Is he at your home?"

"I'm afraid not." Etta turned uphill, nudging her to follow. "Philippe sent me to fetch you. I intended to tell you the news right away, but when I saw your face, Maria, I thought the news might crush what was left of your spirit."

"Etta." Marie caught her breath. "*Please.*"

"Lucas is in jail. Talon just arrested him for murder."

CHAPTER TWENTY-EIGHT

Late afternoon light seeped through the cell window when Lucas heard, from down the hall, the squeal of a door and murmur of a woman's voice.

Marie.

She was finally here.

He hauled himself up from his pallet, ignoring the soreness of his body, as well as the dull pain shooting down his back. He would face his little porcupine while standing on his own two feet. He'd spent the day rolling over in his mind what he needed to say. He was sure she was going to blast him with a mouthful, and he needed his wits about him.

She loomed out of the darkness, and he caught his breath. The last time he saw her, in the hospital, she'd worn a brocade dress that had probably belonged to Etta. Now, buckskin breeches clung to the curves of Marie's thighs. Fringe edged the leather tunic that fell to her hips. Black hair lay loose on her shoulders, tousled like she'd just risen from lovemaking. A weakness spread through him that had nothing to do with his wounds.

She wasn't going to play fair.

"Well, Lucas." She eyed him like she was aiming a flintlock. "You're looking much healthier than when I saw you last."

"You look like you're on a hunt."

"Maybe I am." She raised a brow. "Last time we spoke, you were determined to escape this marriage, after all."

She spoke calmly, but he heard pain behind her words. He'd caused that pain. He deserved the sharpest quills she could shoot.

He said, "Any chance you came to break me out of this cell? It wouldn't be the first time you set someone loose from jail."

"I can't do it this time. Even if I wanted to." She glanced down at his brown woolen breaches that ended too short and raised a brow at the ridiculous, ornately-embroidered waistcoat Philippe had lent him in place of his bloody clothes. "You're a lot bigger than Genny. You won't fit into my clothes."

She was joking with him. His stomach hollowed. What had he been thinking, trying to send this woman away?

With a flick of a hand toward the cell, she added. "You know this is all a ruse, yes? Talon has no intention of charging you with murder."

"So you say." Philippe had repeated the same sentiment, but Lucas had his doubts. "I did kill three men."

"Only two."

He frowned. All three men were dead, he was sure. He'd shot the first one through the window. He'd battled hand-to-hand with Fortin and Landry until both had ended up motionless at his feet. He'd confirmed it before he raised his head to check on Marie, who'd been standing on the porch...holding the flintlock.

"Wait." Spit hit the back of his throat. "You—"

"Turns out I'm a good shot," she interrupted. "I hit what I aimed at. In this case, I aimed at Landry."

His ribs tightened against a rush of feeling. He should have protected her better. It was a great burden to take a man's life, even the life of an enemy. She didn't deserve that burden...yet, at the same time, pride flooded through him. Marie hadn't hesitated. She hadn't flinched. She'd saved him, and herself.

A soldier's daughter.

A soldier's wife.

She said, "Do you think I should confess my crime to Talon? Then he'd throw me in jail right here with you."

"Don't." He gripped the bars of his cage. "Don't put your head in a noose, Marie. Bad enough that mine is in one."

"No judge in Quebec would convict you, Lucas. It was self-defense."

He hoped she was right. He didn't relish the prospect of a trial. Or being away from her for so long.

"Why are we talking about this, anyway?" Her chin puckered in that stubborn way he loved. "The only reason Talon locked you up was because he found out you planned to ship me back to France."

Lucas closed his eyes. Talon had spies everywhere.

"So I'm here to tell you my own news." She paced in a circle in the hall beyond the bars, begging for him to take a long look at the way the deerskin pulled across her plump backside. "I've decided I'm not sailing back to France, no matter what."

Relief hollowed him out.

"I'm staying in Quebec with Etta. If you think you can force me onto a ship, I'll remind you that you'll have no say in the matter once we get an annulment."

The word was like a mule-kick to the gut. How could he have ever thought of separating from her?

"And if we *do* get an annulment," she persisted, "then I'll remain here until a fine young man takes a liking to me—"

"Like hell you will."

The words cut clean through him.

"Then stop me." Her smile turned wicked. "Forget the annulment. Promise you'll keep me as your wife. Then Talon will release you, and we'll be together."

Lucas pressed closer to the bars, wanting to breathe in her scent instead of the prison-wall damp and tang of the wet iron bars between them. He ached to reach through, seize her, and kiss her senseless, but he hadn't yet given her a reason to think he had changed his mind. He wanted to be her husband, now and forever, but they still had one matter of unfinished business.

Dropping his voice, he said, "You shouldn't have done it, Marie."

"Bargain for your freedom with Talon?" She flipped her hair back. "Or threaten to marry another man?"

"You shouldn't have risked the river."

She stilled, swaying back. So Philippe hadn't told her he'd shared the story, or at least enough of the story to jog Lucas's memory.

"I'm more than twice your weight, wife. How the hell did you get me out of that bed, out of the cabin, into the canoe?"

She frowned, hesitated, and then shrugged. "I forced you to walk, though you were half-asleep."

"Forced me?"

"I nudged you awake, urged you out of bed. You fell to your knees a couple of times. I had to brace you upright most of the way."

"It's a wonder your arms didn't come out of your sockets. You could have crippled yourself."

"Don't you remember stepping over the rim of the canoe?"

His mind grasped but found nothing.

"You became alert for a second, long enough to recognize the canoe." She pushed hair off her cheek, and he glimpsed scabs on her knuckles. "You told me not to forget the paddle. It was already in the canoe, but that was the first time you spoke and made any sense."

"Marie." The danger was over, but for him the fear was still raw. "Of all the crazy, reckless——"

"Should I have left you there, feverish and alone?"

"The canoe could have capsized." Her words curled around his heart, but he couldn't help himself. "You could have drowned."

"If I hadn't brought you here, you would have died for sure." Her nostrils flared. "I would risk the danger again, in a heartbeat."

Such words, to come out of all that porcelain prettiness. All the images he'd gathered of her—king's girl, baron's niece, convent orphan, determined sharpshooter, playful hunter in moose-skin breeches—all coalesced into this one petite, iron-spined survivor.

He couldn't imagine a more perfect wife.

"Did you think I wouldn't try to save you?" she said into the silence. "And, having saved you, did you think I'd just let you send me away? How could I spend my life embroidering altar cloths, after all this?" The iron bars rang as she gripped them, too. "I'm staying in this world, Lucas. I will grow squash, beans, and corn. I'll learn to dye porcupine quills and sew them into moccasins. I will scour the woods for berries and roots and learn which ones are good, which ones are poisons, and which ones are medicine. I'm staying here, to make a new life, even if you don't want me to be your wife."

"I want you to be my wife." He shoved his hands through the bars to cup her cheeks. "Haven't you learned never to listen to what a man says while he's in a fever?"

She breathed hard, her gaze fierce.

"You," he said, pressing his head against the bars, "are the bravest, most fearless woman I have ever known."

"You're saying this because your freedom is in my hands."

"It's my heart in your hands."

She made a choked sound.

"I've been a fool, Chepewéssin. I didn't want to acknowledge how strong you've become. I wanted you to be safe above all else, but fighting you is like fighting the north wind."

He kissed her, though it made for an awkward kiss between the bars, broken up by gasps and laughter and shifts of position. She slipped her arms through to run her fingers up his shoulders, avoiding the sore side of the knife wound.

"Forgive me," he whispered. "For underestimating you."

"You acted out of love. You're already forgiven."

"My star maiden. With you, I am healed."

Her joyful, rippling laughter made his chest swell. He felt three times larger than ever before, strong as an ox, flooded with happiness. Were he stomping in the woods around his cabin he felt like he could yank full-grown pines out of the earth by the roots.

"I'll speak to Talon," she whispered, pulling away. "He'll set you free. Then we can go home."

Home.

The future unfurled before him.

Already his mind populated it with dreams.

CHAPTER TWENTY-NINE

Six Months Later

Leaning over the outdoor campfire, Marie ladled a simmering mix of milk, butter, and squash from the iron pot. She poured the soup into one of the scooped-out gourds she'd prepared for today's feast. The fresh scent of pumpkin tickled her nose and made her stomach growl, but as the hostess of the gathering, it wasn't yet her turn to settle down and eat with her many guests.

Cecile's son, Etienne, seized the bowl from her outstretched hand.

"Careful." Marie laughed as Cecile's stepson put the edge to his lips. "The soup is still hot."

Etienne shrugged, took a swig, and closed his eyes in appreciation.

"You've got a mustache," Marie teased, casting a look at Cecile. "Don't let your stepmother see that, or she'll come at you with a razor."

"And I will." Cecile wiped off the mess with a quick finger. "I don't want anyone suggesting my stepson is old enough to go running in the woods."

Etienne ducked his head and set off for one of the trestle tables set up in the clearing. Marie filled another bowl for Ceci. Her friend looked thin and pale, gripped by worry, though she was making a valiant effort to pretend to enjoy the gathering. Marie had been so busy with the preparations, she hadn't had a moment alone with her. Marie wondered if Ceci's trouble lay with the husband who'd refused to join them.

"You and I," Marie said, handing Cecile a bowl, "should take a walk through the woods later, when the men are busy with their pipes. Yes?"

Cecile nodded and then trailed after Etienne, while Marie made a wish for her happiness. Surely, it was possible. Just look at how everything had turned out for her and Lucas, and all the friends they'd gathered for this harvest feast. She watched as they swiped their soup bowls with crusts of bread and pulled meat from turkey bones. The food pleased them, the food she cooked, and that gave her a rush of pride. All around the tables, they laughed and chatted and debated, some dressed in deerskin leggings, some in satin breeches, some wearing beaver hats, others with feathers tied in their dark hair. Among them were French settlers and Huron traders, an Abenaki family coming through to their southern hunting grounds, and a few soldiers who'd spent the summer building small cabins across the river.

The sight of the gathering was like something out of a book she'd never read. A book she was writing herself, in little pieces, in the letters she sent home to Isabelle, one of the little girls at the orphanage. Isabelle was old enough to read the letters aloud to the littler ones. It was someone else's turn, now, to tell fantastic tales about faraway lands and ferry the youngest orphans off to dreamland.

A pair of strong arms slipped around her from behind.

"You've done enough." He tickled her ear with his breath. "Come eat with us."

"You don't like when I play the great lady of the manor?"

"Only in bed."

She laughed and turned around, taking in the full sight of her handsome husband, framed by the maples ablaze beyond his dark, beautiful head.

"I like the way you're looking at me, woman." He pulled her hand to the crook of his elbow and propelled her toward their guests. He'd chosen French clothing for today's event, his Sunday best. He looked like a rather brawny country squire. "When your eyes go soft like that, Marie, I want to drag you inside. But your moans would disturb everyone's dinner."

"Promises." She grinned as they strode toward the benches. "So many promises."

"Speaking of promises." He laid a kiss atop her head. "When were you planning to tell me?"

"Tell you what?"

He paused as they neared the revelers. Hands on her waist, he turned her around to face him. He slid a hand between them, out of sight of their guests, to lay his palm over her abdomen.

"What?" Her mouth fell open. "How…?"

"I know your body better than my own, my love."

It was supposed to be a surprise. She'd only known for a week or so, and they'd been so busy preparing for this gathering she hadn't found the right moment to tell him. It should be a special moment, shouldn't it, when a wife told her husband they were going to have a baby? Now, watching his face, bright with knowledge and mischief, she realigned her thinking and took notice of everything. The slight breeze rustled the leaves. The air that smelled of burning oak, and sweet squash, and pine. The look of love on Lucas's face.

It wasn't only the moment that was sacred.

It was the news that made it so.

"Yes," she finally confessed, laughing. "There's more than bread rising in the home of Captain Lucas Girard."

Barking a laugh, he hauled her up and swung her around, her skirts flying. The chatter at the table dimmed as the men and women watched their display. Her head spun by the time Lucas planted her back on her feet. He held her steady as he walked her to the head of the table and swept up two glasses of apple cider.

"Friends." Lucas raised his glass. "We have much to celebrate. The food on this table. The land beneath our feet. The friends around us. The peace among our neighbors." Around the table came nods and grins and rumbles of agreement. "My wife and I have a very special reason to be grateful."

He touched her again. Gasps rose among the women. The men took a little longer to figure it out, but when they did, they shouted their congratulations. Cecile, at the far end of the table, grasped her throat, tears springing to her eyes.

"Here's to a beautiful world," Lucas toasted her. "And to a new life."

Marie joined the toast, then walked to the far end of the table, running a gauntlet of good wishes, to take the plate that had already been filled for her. Bowing to the urgings of the Huron matriarch seated at her side, Marie ate the choice pieces the woman slipped to her. Platters were passed around and bones licked clean and the air was full of several languages and much laughter. The autumn sun cast dappled shadows over everything. Her heart filled with such gratitude, running over.

After the meal, the men wandered to the riverside where Lucas had set up a circle of logs and a fire pit. The men had much to talk about. Lucas had been planning this gathering for weeks. Marie was proud of her husband for bringing so many different people together, forming a new community to discuss matters of security and mutual needs. The sweet smell of tobacco permeated the air as a peace pipe was shared. Cecile, the settler's wives, and several of the Huron women helped her clear the trestle tables, covering what food that remained, so folks could fill their bellies again if they got hungry. In the late afternoon, a raucous game involving sticks and a deerskin ball began, and Marie had to nurse a few scratches and bumps. When the sun streamed low through the trees, and the men returned in weariness to the fire by the riverbed, Marie turned her attention to the comfort of their guests, many of whom bunked in the wide open, others in the shelter of the barn or the cabin's parlor.

Later that evening, Marie slipped satisfied and weary into bed. Lucas joined her much later, slipping an arm around her midsection. From beyond the bedroom door came the sound of rustling bedclothes, of low whispers, suppressed laughter, and light snoring. For a moment, she was transported back to her orphanage dormitory, that long-ago life. How little of the world she'd understood then.

She'd never imagined the depths of happiness a woman could feel, lying under furs with a loving man's arm across her waist. She burrowed back into Lucas, happy they had so many people around them now, native families that promised to stay a few days as they traveled between hunting grounds, and settlers who would be no more than a mile or two away during the long winter.

She also looked forward to a bit of privacy, if only to have Lucas to herself. His arm tightened as if he'd heard her thoughts. He tickled the nape of her neck with a kiss as his fingers slid under her shift.

She sucked in a breath at his touch.

His laugh was a rolling rumble. "You are awake."

"Very much so, now." Her breath went shallow as he teased her body. "But we have twelve guests in the parlor, Lucas, and not all of them are asleep."

"We'll be quiet. You're quivering against my hand."

Her pleasure tightened. "Maybe I'm just cold."

"Your body says otherwise."

He kissed her on the shoulder and then leaned over so she could look up into his face. She cupped his short-bearded cheek, marveling at the change in him. She could hardly believe the man whose eyes now danced with love was the same stony stranger she'd married that cold day in Quebec.

He pressed his mouth against hers. He tasted of sweet tobacco and desire, of a fierce and sudden need, and she couldn't resist. A little while later, as she struggled to muffle her pleasure, she knew with bright clarity the life in her womb would be a boy. Yes, the baby would be a frolicking, dark-haired boy, born by Easter day.

A low voice came from the other side of the bedroom door.

Etienne, softly calling Lucas's name.

Lucas grunted, still breathing heavily from his own release. "I forgot." He rolled to his back. "I promised Etienne that I'd show him the constellation of Orion the Hunter rising in the sky before I went to bed."

"Don't complain." She snuggled into the pillow. "His timing could have been a lot worse."

"True." He laid a kiss on her forehead. "Today was a good day, an excellent day. But when it comes to you and me, *Anentaks,* winter can't come soon enough."

THE END

Don't miss the other novels in the King's Girls Series

HEAVEN IN HIS ARMS: Book One

Struggling to survive on the streets of Paris, Genny agrees to a dangerous masquerade: She switches places with a King's Girl, a young noblewoman about to be shipped to the colonies. It's a risky venture with a high price—once overseas, Genny must marry a stranger....

ABOUT THE AUTHOR

Lisa Ann Verge is a critically acclaimed RITA© nominated author whose many novels have been published worldwide and translated into seventeen languages.

She started her career writing emotionally intense romance about sexy men and dangerous women, and now as **Lisa Verge Higgins** she also writes life-affirming women's fiction.

A finalist for RT Book awards five times over, Lisa has won the Golden Leaf and the Bean Pot, and twice she has cracked Barnes & Noble's General Fiction Forum's top twenty books of the year.

When not writing, she can be found hunting wild mushrooms, learning Turkish, and keeping track of her three adult daughters, whose adventures make life interesting.

Made in the USA
Middletown, DE
03 April 2022